The Dew
on the Roses

Joyce French Turner

iUniverse, Inc.
New York   Bloomington

The Dew on the Roses

iUniverse books may be ordered through booksellers or by contacting:

iUniverse
1663 Liberty Drive
Bloomington, IN 47403
www.iuniverse.com
1-800-Authors (1-800-288-4677)

Because of the dynamic nature of the Internet, any Web addresses or links contained in this book may have changed since publication and may no longer be valid. The views expressed in this work are solely those of the author and do not necessarily reflect the views of the publisher, and the publisher hereby disclaims any responsibility for them.

ISBN: 978-1-4502-4344-5 (sc)
ISBN: 978-1-4502-4345-2 (ebk)

Printed in the United States of America

iUniverse rev. date: 07/23/2010

The Dew on the Roses

Dedicated to my son Eric Turner for all his help with editing and graphics, to my husband Fred Turner for all his support with this endeavor, to my son Joseph Turner for the word processor to help expedite the writing process, to my granddaughter Amanda Gaddy, and to Rose Turner for all her help and encouragement.

The Waking Home on South 10th Street

CHAPTER I

THE WEDDING 1899

Anna was not beautiful, but certainly attractive for her twenty-three years. Anna had her mothers' complexion, pale gold hair and twinkling blue eyes, depicting her German ancestry. There was nothing small and dainty about Anna. She had a sturdiness and cleanness of line to body and face, brought about no doubt by the walks she took on lovely days and the bicycling through Tenth Street Park. Her hair was always swept up in soft curves in the fashion of the day that Mr. Gibson had made so popular. This morning, there was a garland of fresh flowers pinned to the back, for today was her wedding day.

Anna's sister Caroline had just finished buttoning her white brocade wedding gown with the high frilled collar, and went downstairs to get the corsage of flowers Anna would wear pinned to the bodice of the gown. Anna walked across the room to raise the fringed shade and let the beautiful warm spring air of April seep into the room. It was still quiet in the street below. There had been noise and confusion inside, with the final preparations for the wedding.

Anna was thankful for these moments to be alone, her last time in her own lovely room in the big, warm, cheerful house on Tenth-Street. Memories flooded back, she had been born in this house in 1877. Her mother and father, Hannah and Fred Waking had made the voyage from Germany to join relatives and friends in this lovely and picturesque, up and coming, town of Richmond, Indiana. Her father had been a sailor, but gave up the sea for good and set up shop for plumbing, well drilling and later incorporated a line of sporting goods into his business on Main-Street. This enabled Anna to be the first girl in Richmond to have a bicycle.

She pulled back the lace curtains and drew a deep breath. How could she go through with this marriage? To put her life and future into the hands of another, even though she loved that person very much, it was giving her what everyone called the "jitters". How much did she really know about Lorenzo Dow Boswell anyway? Her thoughts carried her back to the night she first met him at the skating rink.

She had skated and enjoyed her circle of friends and had caught the eyes of a stranger looking at her. He seemed much older than the group she was with that day. When an intermission came, the girls huddled in a corner to talk and gossip about the newcomer. Andrea provided them with the information she had acquired about the "tall, dark, stranger." "He's not from around here, his family farms up around Whitewater. Isn't he handsome though?" She gave him a glance over her shoulder and continued, "I met his sister Floretta, and she doesn't dress like she came off a farm, her clothes look like they came from Paris designers to me. She is the most stylish girl I have ever seen here and the most stuck-up too, I might add." The girls happened to see the fellow approach at that moment, next to an auburn haired beauty dressed in black, which made her figure appear very slim and petite. They talked briefly, and she left as unobtrusively as she had appeared. "Was that his sister?" asked Anna. "NO", replied Andrea, "I've never seen that girl before, I wonder who she is, that's mysterious."

The music started to play again, so the girls went for a new round of skating, when Anna noticed that her skate was loose. Anna had just sat down on a bench to adjust her skate, and then suddenly, the tall, dark and handsome stranger was down on one knee at her feet to assist her. When he asked if he could be of help, Anna looked down at the upturned face and was captivated by the darkest eyes, with such a sparkle, she had ever seen. Everyone in her family and her friends were all blond with blue eyes. Anna was not shy, and the rest of the evening was spent in conversation with Lorenzo Dow Boswell. The name sounded so foreign to her and he had explained that he was named after a stump preacher that roamed the west, by the name of Lorenzo Dow. He was born on the prairie, in the west, around Des Moines, Iowa. The Boswells were Scotch-Irish descent and his father had been an army captain. Anna had in turn rattled off all her names, including her confirmation, "I'm Anna Amelia Margaret Waking. I was born right here in Richmond on Tenth-Street, and I've never been farther from home than Cincinnati, Ohio. I went to school there with my friends for a brief time, but I don't like being away from home for long."

No, she hadn't liked being away from home for long, and now she would be leaving for good. Oh, there would be visits, but it would not be the same. The mornings she spent waking up in her front bedroom, with the massive walnut bed and carved furniture, the soft light coming in from the tall lace curtained window, the sounds of the birds in the maple trees, and a horse clopping by on Tenth Street. The thoughts of her mother in the kitchen, the smell of fresh baked bread, and her father reading aloud from the big German bible every morning at breakfast.

At Christmas, her sisters Mary and Caroline, and her older brothers, Fred and William, although everyone called him Billy, would gather around the massive grand piano in the parlor and sing her favorite song, "0h Tannenbaum." The Christmas tree of which they sang, stood in the front parlor window, fragrant with the very smell of Christmas, adorned with all the ornaments from Christmas past. In this parlor window, she had pressed her face against the frosted pane and had watched the snow fall silently.

Times were always changing; she was the youngest since her little brother Walter had died of lung fever when he was only three years old. That was the only sad memory of her youth. She had missed her sisters and brothers as they had married and left home, but they had not gone far and she saw them almost everyday.

Mary had married first and lived close by on South E. Street. Anna had gone to stay with Mary to help her when she had her first child. Anna was only thirteen at the time, but Mary said she had been a big help to her and wanted to give her something special. She chose a gold ring and had it engraved with an inscription on the inside of the band. Anna was so proud of it; she never took the ring from her finger. Bill had married and went into the business with her father. Fred married his long time sweetheart, Edith, and took a job with the railroad. Caroline was the closest to Anna, and had not been married long herself. She lived close to home on Eleventh-Street. She was there early this beautiful morning to help Anna on her special day.

It had taken a long time to fasten the long row of small covered buttons that ran down the back of Anna's wedding gown. Caroline coming in the door, with the corsage of flowers pulled Anna back from her reminiscence of by-gone years to the present moment. She turned from the window and stepped to the marble topped dresser to pick up a pair of dainty gold and pearl earrings and placed them in her pierced ears. "It's going to be a perfect day, and as warm as June. Wait till you see how lovely the house looks all decorated for your reception. Mary is outside decorating the grape arbor, by the back door, because guests are going to overflow the house. Mama says it is almost time to leave for the church. Do you have your white gloves?" Anna reached for the gloves, taking them from the tissue lined, flat, narrow box from Knollenberg's Department Store. Caroline was chattering away in her excitement of the day, "That's your something new, and Mama gave you her lace fan for something old. You borrowed my lace handkerchief, but what do you have for something blue?" Anna responded with a little laugh and a somewhat whispered confidence, "My something blue is a ribbon that runs through the eyelet lace in my drawers!"

Someone was calling up the stairs that the horse and buggy had been brought around from the livery stable, so with one last look in the mirror that reflected back a lovely bride, and a last look at the room, she closed the door and followed Caroline down the stairs to the waiting family full of hugs, kisses, and wishes for her happiness. Anna slipped out the back door and made her way to the garden, her favorite place. She selected an early bloom of her own to add to her bouquet. She had planted and tended the flower garden, for her it was a touch of heaven on earth. Her favorite hymn was "In a Garden", and she often sang as she worked, "I come to the garden alone, while the dew is still on the roses......." She had a strong faith in God, and she attended church at St. Paul's Lutheran every Sunday, but she felt closer to God here in her garden.

Caroline was calling her anxiously, "Anna, we must be going

now." "I'm coming", and clutching her spring bloom carefully, Anna walked back to the house. Hannah took her bloom and added it to her bridal bouquet while Anna slipped on her elbow length white gloves.

Before the buggy bore the wedding party down the street the few blocks, to the church, Anna took a long last look at the large white two story house, with its side porch and dark green shuttered windows, especially to the window of her room. She would return to this house, but as a married woman, leaving her carefree days of her girl-hood behind. It was somewhat a mixture of leaving the past that made her feel sad, and yet starting a new path into the future with the happy feelings of anticipation and a curiosity as to what was around the next corner in her life. She loved Lorenzo and he had been her choice. Her mother and father had not been so pleased at first because he was twelve years older than she, but her happiness was all that mattered to them and they gave their blessing to the match.

The day passed so quickly, almost like a dream. Their vows were made and then afterward all the congratulations from family and friends. The many gifts were opened, cakes were cut, and punch ladled from a crystal bowl into the shimmering cut glass cups. Guests overflowed the house and into the yard, arbor and porch. The horse and buggy was brought around again, and before she could catch a good breath Anna and Lorenzo was whisked off at a fast pace for their honeymoon at the new Westcott Hotel. Anna could never be sure, but as their buggy had left the front of her home she thought she saw a glimpse of an auburn haired girl sitting in a carriage across the street that looked familiar.

It was to be a short honeymoon, in order for Lorenzo to get back to work on the farm. It would be planting time soon and the fields were being prepared. Lorenzo chose the Westcott Hotel. It was the pride of the city of Richmond, and the stateliest, prettiest, and best arranged hotel in the state of Indiana. It boasted a hundred rooms, and was located at the end of Tenth-Street and Main, so it was a very short journey. Anna had walked there frequently and bought her hats at Miss Porters Millinery shop located in the hotel facing Main-Street.

The Westcott Hotel

Lorenzo brought the horse and buggy to a stop at the entrance on Tenth-Street. It had an ornate wrought iron portico for unloading in inclement weather. Lorenzo handed the reins to a porter, who would ensure it was returned to the livery stable. He helped Anna to alight from the buggy and she took his arm and entered the spacious lobby. Lorenzo stepped to the desk for the key and to register while Anna waited by the wide staircase. She was anxious to be out of the lobby and the prying eyes of the people mingling there. She thought she saw a few men look at Lorenzo and wink an eye.

A bellman led them to their room with their light luggage and left them standing to look about the room. When Anna saw the bed, it suddenly occurred to her that she was going to have to share that bed tonight with Lorenzo. As with so many girls, her wedding plans only went as far as the wedding itself. No one mentioned the wedding night. Young ladies were not spoken to of such intimacies, and it was left to the new husband to deal with it. Anna went about the room, looking it over, on her first visit to a hotel. She removed her corsage and carefully placed it on the bureau. She went to the window to adjust the blind and looked down onto Main-Street.

An interurban car had stopped to let passengers off. The sun glinting, two silver streaks, from the rails up Main-Street. Lorenzo came to the window, to look as well, and placed his arm around her. "Would you like to go down to the lobby, or look through the shops?" "No," she replied, "it's been a big day for us, and I would like to just rest and talk. We don't even need to go out to eat. Mama packed us a nice basket. I was too nervous to eat much before, but I feel like I could enjoy it now." They enjoyed their indoor picnic and talked about the plans they had made for the future.

As Anna prepared for bed, she went behind the decorative screen provided for the purpose of discreet undressing, and put on her bridal nightgown. She had made it herself of fine white cotton and trimmed it with lace. She saw that "Dow," as she liked to call him, had on his nightshirt and was sitting up in bed waiting for her. He folded back the covers for her, as she timidly approached the bed. Moonlight streamed into the room and reflected in the mirror of the bureau. A soft breeze blew through open window stirring the sheer drapery. Dow adjusted his pillow and placed both hands behind his head. "Isn't this a beautiful night?" "Yes it is," she answered. "It has been a perfect day all around. I'm really looking forward to getting settled in our home." Dow took her hand in his. "I hope that you will be happy on the farm. It's what I have always wanted to do." Anna responded by placing her other hand against his face. "I will be happy where-ever, as long as we are together." Talking over the day and making plans on this night began a practice that continued throughout the years. Lorenzo was a smart man, he was gentle and patient and Anna discovered that wonderful mystery that takes place between a man and a woman.

Clayton Hunt's Home and Store

CHAPTER 2

LIFE ON THE FARM

The farm was located near the settlement of Centerville to the west of Richmond. The farm belonged to Lorenzo's sister Iowa, and her husband Clayton Hunt. Clayton had a grocery store on Main-Street in Richmond. They wanted to be close to the business, so they resided in a large brick home on the corner of Ninth-Street and South A-Street. Clayton and Lorenzo had an agreement to farm on shares. The house on the farm was left partially furnished for them.

Lorenzo got the horse and buggy from the livery stable and drove Anna out to their new home. The house was a two story, red brick, with a wide veranda across the front. A comfortable setting of white wicker rocking chairs and settee adorned the porch. Anna stepped through the front door entry and entered the spacious foyer. She had laughingly side-stepped Dow's proposal to carry her over the threshold. A stairway of oak balustrades led to the upper floor. The doorway to the left led to what had originally featured double parlors. The sliding doors still gave evidence of the beautiful cornices that adorned the high ceilings. The "Victorian" period was very strong in this house, from the gold leaf mirror over the mantal and the few pieces of furniture left for them, which consisted of a marble topped table, an old secretary, and a square grand piano with large sturdy legs.

Anna returned to the foyer and climbed the staircase to explore the upper rooms. She chose the room she would like for their bedroom. It contained a very handsome old mahogany bed and a bureau with a serpentine front. The other rooms she gave a hurried glance into and then went back downstairs. On the other side of the foyer, were the dining room, and the kitchen behind it. A huge black iron stove dominated that room with a built-in cupboard with glass doors along one wall, and a large table with massive legs stood in the center of the room. Dow joined her at this time and she asked, "Where is the water?" She was looking in every corner. "Out here on the summer porch," answered Dow, as he opened a back door leading to it. There stood a pitcher pump on a stand with a bucket beneath. "I guess there's not a bathroom either," said Anna. Here was a girl ahead of her time in the city. Since her father and brother were in the plumbing business they had indoor bathrooms in their homes. Leaving by the rear door of the summer porch, Anna's eyes followed the well worn path to the back garden and sure enough, there it stood, the little out-house.

Dow stood beside Anna looking apprehensive, "What do you think?" he asked, "Can you make this a home?" "If you can make this farm produce," she replied. "Will there be enough of everything sharing fifty-fifty with Clayton and Iowa?" she inquired. "It should work out just fine. Dad is giving me a pair of mules and wagon and the use of his implements, and Clayton and I will split on the seed cost. He has the fields ready to plant next month," he assured her. "I will have a lot to learn. I'm a city girl and my education at the Young Ladies Finishing School in Cincinnati did not prepare me for this, but I will run the household and you will run the farm," Anna told him.

Living in the country was a new experience for Anna. As soon as she had her new home settled, she planned to make her rounds to the neighbors and meet them, if they didn't come to call first. "Look Dow, see how nice the clock looks on the mantel," Anna exclaimed. She was referring to the Seth-Thomas clock her parents had given them, as a token of their beginning time together, as well as a wedding gift. It chimed out the hour as she spoke, as if it knew it was included in the conversation. "I have such fun finding just the right place for all the gifts we received," she joyfully said. The grand piano stood in one corner of the main parlor, and Anna had found a fringed shawl for the top of it. A tall thin crystal vase of carnations, and her wedding portrait had also been added to it. Anna ran her slim fingers over the ivory keyboard, "Come play a duet with me before I start preparing our supper?" she asked. Dow accepted the invitation and the old house resounded with one lively tune after another.

Anna mastered the big, black, kitchen range trying out recipes handed down from her mother along with some new ones. She planted a kitchen garden and bordered it with Zinnias and other cut-flowers. In a separate, special garden, she grew her Roses. Besides tending garden and taking care of her other everyday tasks, she became very friendly and social with the neighborhood farm women. Anna quickly became a favorite among them.

A day started early on the farm. Anna told her family, in town, that she was up with the chickens. The roosters would crow at the crack of dawn, the time she would get up, dress, and go down to the kitchen to feed the range several sticks of firewood. The range burned night and day, having a reservoir for hot water. Her early mornings had become a routine but on this particular morning, it was different. She brought out a heavy iron skillet as usual and started bacon frying while she selected the largest eggs from the crock. No sooner had she cracked the eggs and put them into the skillet, when her stomach seemed to churn, and she felt terribly ill. She jerked the skillet from the fire and ran out to the backyard. She grabbed onto the clothesline post to hold for support, feeling the nausea gradually subside. "What is wrong with me?" she thought back, "I've never been one for ill health, it couldn't have been anything I ate, I haven't had breakfast yet." Nor did she want any after that episode. She saw Dow coming from the barn, so she hurried back into the house and put the food onto his plate, trying not to look at it, as she done so.

Dr. Bond's Home and Office

The next morning the nausea appeared again. When this feeling continued, she decided to visit Dr. Bond on her next trip into town. She told none of her plans to see the doctor. She was nervous as she entered his office. After a few embarrassing questions, he informed her that she would be having a baby the latter part of January. Anna left the office in a daze. She knew people had babies all the time. She just hadn't known much about the process of the begetting of one or even now the birthing of one. It was not a subject that was discussed, and when it was, it was a whisper. She had not paid much attention. She had not had time to adjust to being a wife yet, and now to become a mother so soon. How would she tell this news to Dow? They had never even spoken of children.

Fortunately she was able to cook other meals of the day with no trouble at all, so she went out of her way to have a special dinner prepared. She put candles on the dining table instead of the customary oil lamp. Dow sat down across from her and surveyed the dining table. "Are we having company?" he inquired. Anna smiled at him across the table and replied, "Well, you could say that I suppose." Then she broke into her discussion of family by asking, "Dow, would you prefer a boy first, or a girl, or would it matter which?" He answered her with a knowing grin on his face, "whatever you decide to give me. When will our little "company" arrive?" "In January," she told him.

By September, Anna was showing herself to be in the family way, so she was content to spend her time in the garden or resting on the porch. Then Christmas came and Anna did what she could to make the house appear festive for the holiday. She could not make a trip to see her family for her time was getting close. On the eve of Christmas, all of her family made the trip to visit her. Then the winter really set in, with cold, dark, and dreary days. These were the worst, and Anna was counting the days.

On January 26, 1900, Dow came into the kitchen after

removing his snowy boots and heavy coat. He had been longer at the barn than normal, getting his livestock warmly bedded in clean straw. He found the kitchen in preparation for their evening meal, but Anna was not in sight. "Anna," he called, and not receiving an answer, went through the house looking for her. He found her in bed, the room dark. "What's the matter Anna, are you sick?" he inquired. "No, not sick," she answered, but my back hurts terribly. I was waiting for you to come in to tell you, I think we should send for the doctor." "I'll go right away," as he hurried out the door. Anna lay there in pain, not knowing exactly what agony she would have to bear to bring her first-born into the world. Dow returned with the doctor trailing soon behind him. Anna was in pain, and Dow paced the floor aware of her suffering. At last, the ordeal was over and Anna and Dow smiled down on their husky little boy. Anna was so pleased with him; she soon forgot the pain and discomfort he had caused her to bring him into the world. Dow reached for the family bible and entered the date and the name they chose, Leonard Paul. Family and friends came to see the new baby as soon as weather permitted.

On Valentines Day, Dow brought a stack of mail into the kitchen. They sat at the table and opened the many cards that came for the baby and Valentines for them. Dow picked up one envelope, looked at the handwriting on it, and without opening it, got up and threw it in the stove and watched the flames consume it. "What was that?" asked Anna. "Nothing," he replied, "just a piece of trash." He handed her several pieces of mail to finish opening and he poured them a fresh cup of coffee from the blue granite pot on the stove. It was obvious that he wasn't interested in Valentines anymore. Leonard cried and Anna went to tend him.

The days passed so quickly with so much that had to be done. The new baby required a lot of care, but she enjoyed rocking and singing to him. She also enjoyed all his firsts, his first smile, rollover, crawl, and step. Fourteen months after Leonard, on March 26th, 1901, Anna gave birth to their second son. They named him Wayne Palmer. In contrast to his brother, who favored Lorenzo, Wayne was blond with blue eyes like Anna. Anna said her days went by like a whirlwind with all the activity the two little boys brought to the household.

CHAPTER 3

CIRCUS DAY 1902

Anna was clearing the breakfast table. Dow had left for the day to attend a cattle auction. It promised to be a lovely spring day. Anna went to the sunny kitchen window to open it and let in the fresh spring air, looking out, she saw the buggy with Caroline driving the horse herself, and her little son Harold perched on the seat next to her. Anna ran to open the back door to greet her sister, "what brings you out so early in the morning?" Caroline and her son entered the cheerful red and white kitchen and responded, "It's circus day! I didn't think you knew, being so far out from town and all, so I came out to get you and the boys to spend the day at the circus with me and Harold." "Oh Carrie, I would love it, but Dow has gone to a cattle auction, and I shouldn't leave without him knowing, and besides, I don't have the extra money to spend. I don't know much about farming, but from the way Dow has been talking, I don't think the farm is producing as well as he thought it would," Anna confided. Carrie was not going to accept her refusal and continued, "Oh come on Anna, we will be back home before Dow gets back, he won't even know you left, and I've got the money for the tickets. I meant to tell you. This outing is my treat."

Caroline had married William Bennett, a proprietor of a cigar store on Main-Street, and they lived in a large comfortable home on Eleventh-Street not far from the business. Evidently it was a profitable business because they seemed to be comfortably well off.

Anna didn't need any further coaxing. She ran to change her dress, adjusted her large straw hat, with the trimmings of bright red cherries on it, and grabbed a pair of white gloves from the small top drawer of her oak dresser. She loved to go places, anywhere, just to be out-and-about, and this would be a wonderful outing. She hurried to the boy's room, pulled each a clean waist from their wardrobe and told them what a treat they were in for today.

It was the best day Anna had enjoyed in a long time. She had been kept home for so long during her two pregnancies, because a lady didn't go out in public during her confinement. As Anna had stated, "that's a good name for it because I was certainly confined." There was also a lot of work involved in running a farm, not that she would be involved with the large animals, or go into the fields. It did, however, spill over into her housework, with the washing of milk containers and such after the milking was done each day. She also fed the chickens and gathered the eggs as part of her daily routine. As with most young girls, she had not thought much past the wedding day. She had helped her mother at home, but it was quite different to have the responsibility for attending the entire household yourself. She kept busy from morning to night, with just the daily chores of cooking, cleaning, washing, ironing and mending. With each child came more to tend.

Today she felt like a bird out of a cage. She was feeling like that young girl, she once was, back on Tenth-Street. They strolled through the circus grounds, watching the tents go up and the animation of each participant going through their routine task so perfectly. The circus was only in town for a day. It moved at night and each morning it was the same routine for them in a different town, but for the towns-people to watch, it was a fascinating process. The circus was a world unto itself. Anna and the boys watched the huge elephants push and pull to raise the tall wooden poles of the big top, sometimes even under the direction of a small dark-skinned boy. They saw clowns in different stages of make-up, and the cook tent where the performers and workers ate their meals. Carrie had brought along a picnic basket of sandwiches, cakes, bottles of milk for the boys, and lukewarm tea for herself and Anna. Carrie spread the lap-robe from the buggy in the shade of a nearby oak tree and they continued to watch the circus goings-on from a distance while they enjoyed their picnic lunch.

The first performance was to start at one o'clock. The boys were already starting to imitate some wild animal sounds they had heard coming from the cages of the wild jungle animals. It was a thrilling performance of bareback riders and high wire acts, with beautiful spangled, sparkling costumes and funny outrageous clowns. The sights, sounds, and smells of the circus is exhilarating to all that come in contact with it and this day worked like a tonic on Anna. They bought popcorn and fresh roasted peanuts in red and white striped bags, and ring master whips in bright colors for each of the boys.

When Anna walked back into her kitchen, she found things as she had left them, none the worse for her leaving the house for the day. She was putting the finishes touches to their evening meal when Dow walked into the room. Anna was singing a catchy tune and her eyes were twinkling with a merry light. The boys were down on their hands and knees growling and cavorting across the floor with imitations of strange animal sounds. Dow laughed and said, "I don't have to ask what you've been up to today, you've been to the circus!"

CHAPTER 4

FLO'S WEDDING

The long buggy ride to the Whitewater farm of her in-laws had been tiring for Anna, especially since she suspected she may be in the family way again, but she didn't want to miss out on the good times a wedding provided. Dow's sister Flo was marrying Orville Rhoads, a wealthy plantation owner from Mississippi and going there to live. This visit would also give her the chance to get to know Dow's family better. The last time she had spoken to some of them was at her own wedding.

The large brick farm house was overflowing with guests and family members coming from all sections of Wayne County. Dow had just lifted her down from the buggy, when she saw her mother-in-law come out onto the porch to welcome them. Kiziah must have been a beauty in her youth, because she was still an attractive woman at her advanced age. Having borne seven children, she was slim and erect in a most fashionable dress of the day. Her skirts rustled as she crossed the porch, the dress being of silk taffeta with high puffed sleeves and a high lace collar that came up to cover a large portion of her neck, with her head

held high above it. Her dark hair with only a slight touch of grey
swept up atop her head and held with fancy combs. She wore long,
dangling garnet earrings in her pierced ears. Her complexion was
still smooth and lovely, her eyes dark and piercing. She had just a
hint of cleft chin, and a soft smile.

Dow had told Anna how his grandfather had teased his father
about going out to find a wife and bringing home a wolf, because
her last name had been Wolfe, spelled with an "E" on the end.
Anna in her own thoughts, but would never speak of this aloud,
could picture her father-in-law more as the wolf for he had a long
and shaggy beard that hid most of his face. She was glad Dow
chose to be clean shaven even though it was the vogue of the day
to wear a mustache.

Dow had paid his mother a brief greeting and after the boys
were lifted down to their mother and grandmother, he gave a flick
of his hands to the reins and started the horses down the drive to
the barn-yard to be fed and watered after they had cooled down
and rested from their long journey. Dow always took the best of
care with his livestock.

Anna knew she was on her own to meet and greet his relatives.
It would probably be a while before he returned to the house.
Fortunately, the first of Dow's sisters to come out onto the porch
was Margaret, everyone called her "Mag". She gave Anna and
the boys each a hug and along with her mother and welcomed
them into the house. The entrance hall was cool and inviting,
after experiencing the heat of the noonday sun. She glanced into
the double parlors to her left, filled with a chattering crowd of
family, and from the dining room further to the rear of the house
somewhere, she heard the rattle of silverware and the click of
china as the dining table was being laid for dinner. Mag ushered
her straight up the mahogany staircase, to an upper floor room,

where she could freshen up after the long dusty ride. Kiziah had taken possession of the boys.

Mag had an outgoing personality much like Anna's, so she felt a kindred spirit between them despite the fact that Mag was so much older. Mag had been married twice. The first husband had died young. During her second marriage, she had two sons almost Anna's age. The eldest son, Claude had brought his young fiancé, Minnie, to the wedding. Mag started to exchange family gossip with Anna, as she removed her hat and gloves, and applied a cool wet cloth to her face, "George is here, came all the way from Dayton. We hadn't seen the twins since they were babies. You know George and Winfield were so close, it was almost like having twins, Mama would say. She never sees George but for it reminding her of Winfield too and he was just a child when he died. Mama doesn't take a loss well at all". "Iowa is in the family way again, did you know?" Mag whispered, looking around and over her shoulder to be sure no one else could pick up on this bit of news. "She sure spoils those other two she has, but then they can afford it if it doesn't do them harm. Mama has spoiled Flo as well, as the rest of us, but her being the youngest, I guess it worked the worse on her, she has taken on some high caflootin' ways. We can't keep up with her these days; anyway, I thought you might have known about Iowa being you're living out there on their farm and all." "No, I didn't," replied Anna, applying some face powder with a large velour puff she had brought along in her carry-all. "I don't see much of her at all except once in awhile at the store, while taking in eggs to sell. Dow lets me take charge of the chickens and the egg money is mine." "If you're ready, we'll go down now and see the family. I think dinner should be ready pretty soon," Mag stated, and led the way downstairs to the crowed parlor.

Dow and his father were standing by the ornate mantle-piece

having a discussion about farming no doubt. That seemed to always be the main topic of conversation in the family among the men folk. Dow looked very handsome in his dark navy suit. Anna noticed he had removed his jacket, but as his usual habit, continued to wear his vest. His father was dressed almost identical, but had kept his jacket intact. He was of larger stature than Dow, with seriousness to his features that bespoke life was not taken too lightly with him. He had suffered the hardships of the pioneer on the western prairie.

An announcement was made from the entrance of the parlor that dinner was ready. Her father-in-law offered his arm to take her in to dinner and Dow nodded his approval and said that he would check on their sons. He knew they were with all the other children having a picnic style dinner at a long trestle table in the yard. The children were being supervised by the ladies from the neighboring farms that came to help. Dow joined Anna at the long table in the dining room. His father at the head of the table asked the blessing, and for awhile, until the passing of many platters and bowls had stopped, Anna had not had a chance to survey the long table as to who was in attendance there. She was accustomed to large family dinners and lots of food, but on the farm there was an abundance of all the produce grown upon it. The dinner table giving evidence to this, with the variety of vegetables consisting of mashed potatoes dotted with home churned butter, bowls of corn, peas, green beans, and platters of fresh ripe tomatoes sliced on a bed of garden lettuce. Large platters of golden fried chicken, fresh from their poultry yard, centered on their table, along with, baked ham and tender roast beef from their last butchering.

As the baskets of fresh, baked, bread was passed, a reference was made by someone, but Anna didn't see who it was. She knew Kiziah Boswell was proud of her freshly baked bread, and had heard the story from Dow, about the time the Indians came to their home on the prairie, while Kiziah was baking the bread. She hadn't let the Indians see her fear and shared her bread dough with them. The Indians had come back later in the day in a fury, and angrily thrust the bread dough back into her hands. It had been handled by every member of the tribes dirty hands from the looks of it, but she tore off a bit of the dough and ate it to show them it was not poisoned. Then she showed them how to bake it, and gave them a loaf of the freshly baked bread from her mornings baking. The Indians had been friends with them from that time on. Kiziah was always reminded of it, at these special occasions, when her bread was passed around the table. Dow would always add the part about the Indians finding him under the bed hiding from them and calling him a "papoose."

As Anna looked down to the opposite end of the table, there sat her mother-in-law, every inch a fine lady, in her silk dress and jewelry. It was hard to think of her as the pioneering woman of the prairie, with all the hardships they went through. She had given Anna a memento of her earlier life, a small wooden needle case she had carried with her when they had crossed the prairie in a covered wagon. To look into those dark piercing eyes you knew this was a woman of spirit and determination and could get through what she must.

Flo was seated next to Orville, her intended husband at Kiziah's right. Anna thought Flo resembled her mother more so than Mag or Iowa. Flo had the piercing dark eyes, except hers didn't have that hint of fun or mischief about them. Kiziah could catch you off guard with her unpredictability sometimes. Conversation around the dinner table went from farm prices as usual to the future plans of Flo and Orville.

A light dessert was brought in because wedding cake would

be served soon. When everyone had eaten so much that they felt sleepy, Kiziah proposed that they get some rest before it was time to leave for the church. The wedding was set for two o'clock at the small village church in Whitewater. There would be a reception with wedding cake and punch. In the late afternoon, the bride and groom would catch a train in Richmond that would connect in Cincinnati, Ohio and then to points further south to Mississippi.

Flo went to her room with several others following her, while those with children went to tend to them. Anna was with this group. Her boys having other children to play with were fine, so she found a comfortable wicker rocking chair under a shade tree in the yard. Iowa joined her, along with Myrtle, the young wife of Mathew, the Boswell's youngest son. Myrtle perched on one end of a wicker settee, while Iowa chose the comfort of the other rocker. How are things out on the farm Anna? Have you gotten used to farm life by now?" Iowa wanted to know. Anna replied, "I'm doing as well as expected I suppose. I tend the house and now I have taken over the chickens. I find I don't mind them at all; in fact, I really enjoy the baby chicks. I just can't bring myself to killing a rooster when I plan a chicken dinner. I have to leave that to Dow." Iowa just shook her head, while timid Myrtle agreed with Anna whole heartedly. "This is such a lovely place, if I were Flo I wouldn't want to leave here. I remember how I felt leaving my home on Tenth-Street," Anna reminisced. Iowa shrugged, "Flo won't miss it one bit, she has big ideas about how she is going to live in Mississippi on that plantation and play the lady of the manor to the hilt." Anna thought Iowa was doing a pretty good job of that living right there in Richmond, and perhaps hated to be bettered by her sister. Competition was rather keen between the two sisters as it was.

Kiziah came out to sit a few minutes on the settee with Myrtle, and announced it was time to leave for the church. She had just left Flo, and as organized as that prim and proper girl was, had everything under control. There was no nervous "jitters" for her! She knew exactly what she was after and she was getting it. All her plans had come off without a hitch. Anna collected Leonard and Wayne, wiped their faces, combed their hair and changed their waists for clean ones she had brought.

The ride to the church was a dusty one, with so many buggies and conveyances using the road at the same time. The dust didn't settle before it was kicked up again. The ceremony was quiet and swift. The groom looked as if he had won the prize of a lifetime. Flo looked beautiful; she was a beautiful girl to start with, besides having a flair for choosing the right clothes and the figure to set them off. Today she was simply breathtaking in white lace. Flo loved lace and the wedding gown was entirely of lace from bodice and sleeves to the tip of the train. Anna overheard one overbearing man laugh and say, "It looked like she had stolen all the lace curtains from every window in the house. She hoped no one else had overheard his remark or there would be hell to pay. The Boswells were not a family to make jest of, for it would not be forgotten and paid back in future.

As soon as it was polite to leave, once Flo and Orville had left for the depot, Anna and Lorenzo started their homeward journey. Kiziah had begged them to spend the night, but Anna was eager to return to her own home. Dow, especially, never wanted to be away overnight. He never visited much on Sundays or holidays. As they rode along, Anna thought back over the day. She had really enjoyed herself. One thing kept nagging at her though. She was trying to remember where she had seen that red haired girl before. Anna had noticed that she sat in the last row at the church, but didn't recall seeing her after that. She just looked familiar, but she couldn't remember from where. That night, after finally getting settled into bed, Anna told Dow how much she liked his sister Mag. "Dow, I'm pretty sure we're going to have another baby, and if it's a girl, I would like to name her Margaret after your sister." The next year, on March 14th, 1903, Anna gave birth to a beautiful baby girl and they named her Margaret Jesse. Mag was very pleased.

Baby Margaret

CHAPTER 5

THE LUNCHEON

It was mid-morning, Iowa and Clayton left the farm for an early visit to discuss farm business. On their way, they stopped by the neat, well kept, farm house to visit Anna. As they were ushered into the parlor, Anna explained that she was in the midst of preparing all her little ones for the ladies luncheon over at a neighboring farm. "How do you expect to manage that Anna?" Iowa asked. "How can you take three children, aged five, four and two, to a luncheon and expect to have a good time, not to mention being seen out, when it is obvious that you are expecting again?" Iowa inquired. Her own little two year old girl, they had named Jesse, was fussing and fidgeting on her lap as she spoke. Anna just laughed as she explained to her, "if I didn't take them with me, I'd never get to go anywhere; besides, they're pretty good children most of the time. In fact, the boys are so shy anymore, they won't leave my side and Margaret stays on my lap. I don't think anyone will even notice my condition; they'll just think I'm putting on weight." "Well, I'm glad you're up to it, I'm sure I'd never be," Iowa remarked. Anna was quick to agree, but she never gave voice to her thought.

Anna thought about it all later, when she was telling Dow about the luncheon. It had become a habit for her to talk over the day's happenings, after they were settled in their bed for the night. "I wonder what Iowa would have done if she had been in my situation this afternoon. The table was set to perfection, with the table cloth that draped all the down to the floor and then tied up on each corner with a large bow. The food was really wonderful too. Margaret sat on my lap, as I knew she would, without any trouble. The boys each had a chair at the table on each side of me. As the plates were placed in front of them, they both slid under the table. I didn't say a word to them, but pretty soon I felt a tug at the hem of my dress. When I looked down at them, they asked me to hand them something to eat because they were hungry. I told them, no, you get nothing to eat under the table. If you're hungry you must sit at the table and eat properly with everyone else. The hunger overcame their shyness, and they finally came up to sit at the table and enjoyed their lunch," Anna laughed softly at the remembrance of the afternoon. Dow reached over and found her hand in the darkness, and squeezed it gently, "Anna, you always handle the situation, whatever comes along."

"Something is in the wind", thought Anna. "Dow goes through the mail and throws unopened letters in the stove and calls it trash. He doesn't want to go anywhere, even dreads going to the feed store. This afternoon I'm going to insist he drive me into town for my shopping. I'll tell him I don't feel like driving myself; after all, I am several months pregnant again."

After lunch, Dow hitched up the horse and buggy and lifted his three spic-and-span children one by one into the rear seat. Anna came out of the house and down the walk, looking beautiful in her lavender organdy dress, with large picture hat to match. She loved to dress up and go places. It was a lovely spring day to be out and about. They traveled down National-Road, and across the Main Street Bridge. They passed the grandeur of the large stone Court House and her fathers plumbing shop across from it, on the opposite side of Main-Street. Her destination today was Knollenberg's Department Store for yard goods. She needed diaper material to hem and some soft flannel, to make warm gowns. This would be an October baby. Dow pulled up on the reins, and the horse stopped a short distance down from the store. In the last available space, near the store, he helped Anna to alight. She spoke to the children, "we'll get a treat when I get back. I won't be long."

Anna entered the large store. Yard goods were located at the far back. She enjoyed looking at all the other wares on her way. After making her purchases and leaving the store, she saw the buggy down the street. Dow was standing by the horse talking to, of all people, that red-haired woman she had seen several times before. As she approached the buggy, the woman hurriedly walked away. Dow took her packages and helped her up into the buggy. "Who was that lady?" Anna asked. "She looks so familiar, I've seen her before but I just can't place her." "We'll talk about that later," Dow said, as he picked up the reins. "Did you get what you were looking for?" "Yes I did, and some even on sale," said Anna. "Let's take the children for some ice cream now."

That evening, when they had settled in for the night and talked over their day, Anna asked about the red-haired woman. Dow began, "She was a friend of Flo's. She kept asking me to take her places and I refused her. I've never given her encouragement. She writes the love letters that I won't read anymore; the ones I burn up. I should have told you a long time ago, but I thought she would give up and quit pestering me, especially after we were married and now have three children. I never wanted anything to upset you. You were either pregnant, or about to be. She never would take No for an answer. She's like a clinging vine that I can't get rid of." "Sounds more like Poison Ivy to me," Anna told him. "Well, don't let it worry you any more; we'll see it through together." "You're one in a million, Anna. It was lucky for me that I went to the skating rink the night I met you. I almost didn't go because I was afraid she would be there." Anna thought to herself, "Avoiding a problem doesn't solve it. Sometimes you've got to take the bull by the horns, and she knew she would!"

CHAPTER 6

THE BITTER AND THE SWEET

On a beautiful, crisp, October morning in 1905, Anna gave birth to a fine baby boy. She named him Frederick Harl. She knew her father would be pleased to have a grandson named for him, and her brother was named Fred also. She was tired, and very grateful for all the help she had been given by her sisters and also Mag. It was Mag that broke the news to her, that baby Fred was not absolutely perfect. Two of his fingers on his left hand were webbed together. Dow came to her bedside and held her as she cried. "It's not that bad Anna; it can be fixed. Doctors can separate them; at least, it's not his right hand.

As it came to be, it was Anna that would be the patient for the doctor. The first morning she was able to get up and get dressed; she looked closely at herself in the big mirror above her dresser. She thought her neck looked swollen. With the passing of a few weeks, she began to discover a lump that was forming on her throat. On her first visit into Richmond to see her mother and father, they insisted that she consult a doctor that very afternoon. Anna was never able to forget the hopeless feeling, sitting in the doctor's office, hearing that she had a goiter on her neck. It was something that they couldn't do anything about and would probably increase in size. She thought it was terrible and unsightly. She left the doctor's office with her scarf draped high around her neck. The same she had done when she arrived and continued to do so, whenever she would be seen in public.

Anna's father had heard of electrical treatments that could be given, and sent Anna to an expensive specialist. He paid for it himself; knowing Dow didn't have the money required for it. Anna was faithful to maintain her treatments, but to no avail, the lump continued to grow larger with time. Anna didn't have time to wallow in self-pity. Her days were occupied with caring for her four children, attending church, and helping her neighbors whenever she was needed. The only indication she gave that the goiter bothered her, was to be sure she had a scarf around her neck when she dressed to go out.

On Christmas Eve, the family gathered together in the parlor, of the big tenth-street house. Anna's father gave her a very special Christmas gift, a fur scarf! Anna thought she had never seen such a beautiful thing, as she stroked the soft, glossy brown fur. This was a wonderful Christmas and one she knew she would never forget.

Spring had come at last, and Dow was in the front yard mowing grass. Anna took the children upstairs for their afternoon nap. The warm breeze was blowing the sheer curtains in the open window. Anna walked to the window to adjust the shade and looked out onto the front yard and drive. Anna couldn't believe her eyes. A buggy had turned into their drive and the red-haired woman she had seen and heard about held the reins of the horse. "My, she is getting bold, coming to our home," Anna said to herself. She noticed Dow had stopped his mowing and was shading his eyes to see who was coming down the drive. When the buggy stopped at the hitching post, at the entrance to the wide walkway, which led to the porch, Dow slowly approached it.

Anna was angry, very angry! She left the window and started down the stairs. When she reached the foyer, she saw the buggy whip, in the brass umbrella stand, at the side of the front door. She grabbed the whip, and banged the screen door behind her, as she headed towards the buggy and the red-haired woman. "What do you want here Miss?" Anna asked. "I'm Hazel, a friend of Lorenzo," the red-haired woman answered. "It takes two to form a friendship," Anna told her. "If you don't understand what he has told you, I will make it very plain, don't come back. Don't send letters and don't sneak around to try and see him, or I'll take this buggy whip and teach you a lesson about leaving my husband alone!" Anna then flicked the whip at the horse's flank and it started off. Hazel quickly grabbed the reins, her face so pale, it made the red of her hair stand out even more. The horse moved at a brisk pace down the drive and onto the road.

Anna looked at Dow standing there, starting to recover from his shock, seeing Anna in a fury with the buggy whip. He grinned and shook his head, "I had no idea what a "Tiger" I married." Anna laughed, "Didn't you know all women become "Tigers" to protect their home and family? Let's go sit on the porch; I'll bring us some cold lemonade. It's a hot day, we can relax and cool off."

Threshing Machine

CHAPTER 7

THE HARVEST

Anna woke up extra early on this important day. She went to the window and pulled aside the lace curtains to get a good view of the fields, and a sign that it was going to be a fine day. It was, and she said, "Thank You Lord." She hurried down to the kitchen and started on another day of cooking. She had been baking pies, cakes, and cookies for the last two days. She wanted to be sure there would be enough food for the threshing gang. Dow had gone, to the barn, to do the feeding and milking. Breakfast, this morning, was a quick bite of whatever was handy. In Anna's case, it was a slice of bread and butter and a hot cup of coffee. She would be sampling tastes, of her cooking, all morning and knew that would sustain her. She got a pot of snap beans started, and made several batches of doughnuts. At last, all the food was prepared and ready to serve to the threshers, as they came in from the fields, for the noon meal. The ladies, from the neighboring farms, in the community came to help serve the trestle tables, set up in the yard. During threshing time, they moved from farm to farm, helping each other to get their crops in.

Anna put Margaret, her three-year-old and ten month old Frederick, down for early naps, hoping they would sleep through the noise in the yard. Six year old Leonard and his five year old brother, Wayne, had slipped into the kitchen. Seeing the platter of sugar covered doughnuts on the table, they both reached for a doughnut from the platter. Mrs. Pringle, who had grudgingly come to help, from a distant farm, had just entered the kitchen. The other ladies were setting the long trestle tables in the yard. When she saw the boys with the doughnuts, she approached them clapping her hands, "No-No, put those back now, they're not for you!" The boys stared at her with puzzled looks on their little faces. It happened at the moment Anna was returning to the kitchen. Her temper flared, "You hold on there lady, I provided all this food. I made those doughnuts and my boys can have all they want!" She walked over to the platter, and handed each of the boys another doughnut for their other hand, and led them to the door. "Go out and play now," she said to them in a quiet voice. Turning back to Mrs. Pringle, and raising her voice Anna said, "Get out of my kitchen, I don't need your help here!" Mrs. Pringle started removing her apron as she headed for the back door with her nose in the air. Anna sat down on the nearest kitchen chair. She was worn out from the morning work, and now shaken from the episode with Mrs. Pringle. "I don't know what Dow is going to make of this, but I couldn't help myself. I had enough of that bossy woman," she said to herself.

The ladies were coming into the kitchen for the food to place on the tables outside. Anna got back on her feet and followed them outside, as she took a bowl of green beans and a platter of fried chicken, to the tables of hungry men. She hoped that there would be a good crop this year to make a profit for them. The men ate and enjoyed the bounty of good food served to them. Then they returned to the fields to continue their farm-work. The ladies cleared the tables and washed the dishes. Anna's next door neighbor noticed Mrs. Pringle wasn't among them, and commented on it. "I asked her to leave," Anna remarked, and added, "no one bosses my kitchen or my children either."

When Dow finally returned to the house that evening, they sat down to a late supper. Anna had put aside a meal, in the warming oven, from the noon preparation. She told him about Mrs. Pringle, and then turned the conversation to the crop. "How does it look? Will we make something on it this year?" Dow took a long sip of his coffee before he answered, "Not what I had hoped it would make. Let's go to bed now, I'm just too worn out to think about anything more tonight."

Fall was in the air, a beautiful time of the year. The leaves were turning red and gold. The crops were in, such as they were. Farming didn't come with a guarantee, some years were good and some were not. Anna thought that most of them were not. The seven years spent on the farm and it didn't seem to be very prosperous. Anna made up her mind that she would talk to Dow about leaving the farm. She got the children off to bed, and then proceeded to their room, setting the lamp on the bureau, and pulling down the shade at the open window. She quickly undressed and put on her white cotton nightgown. It was one she had made herself for her bridal trousseau with trim she had crocheted. As she was turning down the covers on the bed, Dow came into the room. "I need to talk to you about something very important to me." "All right," Dow replied, "I knew something was in the wind."

Anna sat down on the bed and began, "Papa has cancer, and he kept it from us as long as he could, but it has gotten worse and he will soon be at the point where he won't be able to leave his bed. Mama isn't doing well herself. Her legs are swelling and painful if she's on her feet too long. She's going to need help with him, and she has asked if we will move in with them. I know it's a great deal to ask of you, I know you enjoy farming." She looked at him, wondering what he was going to say. She would be so happy to go back to town, to the lovely big house on Tenth-Street.

He came and sat down beside her, putting his hands on his knees, as he always did when he was pondering a problem. "Well, there's no question about it, we must do what has to be done," Dow replied. "It's not as if this farm was ours. Iowa can get a tenant farmer. We can settle on what stock and crops we have, and then sell what we don't need. I can get a job in town, maybe help your brother, Bill, in the plumbing shop once in awhile." Anna put her arms about his neck and hugged him. I should have known you would understand how much I wanted to be there for Mama and Papa in their time of need. Long after the lamp had been blown out, they lay awake, talking and making plans for arranging the move to town.

CHAPTER 8

THE NEW BEGINNING

In a short time, Anna, Dow and their children settled into the big Waking family home on South Tenth-Street. Anna and Dow shared the room that had been Anna's, in her girlhood days. Many mornings, she awoke and felt the gladness of being home again. Sometimes she even felt like that young girl again, but then she would hear a child's voice call out, and reminded that she had four children of her own, in those other rooms upstairs.

The children were enrolled in school, and attended Sunday school at St. Paul's Lutheran Church on South Seventh-Street. Despite her father's illness, he still read his German bible every morning at breakfast. Margaret decided she wanted to be called "Peggy" now. She would sit and listen to her grandfather's stories for hours. Caroline's daughter, Marjorie, came to play and listened also.

Everything seemed to be working out very well. Dow was learning the plumbing business, the children were happy, and Anna was very content. Neighbor's stopped in frequently to pass the time of day. Hannah and Fred were doing so much better with her there. The family was close again. Mary and Caroline were there often to sew and exchange recipes. Their brother Fred would come by to sit on the porch and entertain Leonard and Wayne, and little Fred. When in season, he fed them cherries from the tree in the yard, and they dearly loved him. Anna was "expecting" again. She spent her summer days in the garden with her roses, with the sounds of the birds chirping in the trees, and children at play. Dow had insisted she get more rest. She had been quite ill at times; this time things were not going so well.

CHAPTER 9

THE RUSH FOR THE DOCTOR

The August evening was hot and humid; Anna had somehow got the dishes done and the children off to bed. They called these "dog days" but she didn't know why. She had not felt well at all today. She had awakened that morning with her head pounding, and the heat of the day hadn't helped any. She felt wilted and weak as a kitten. Dow was out on the porch, hoping to feel a little cooler night air. Anna walked to the screen door to join him on the porch, when a slight shiver ran through her, as a veil of blackness overcame her and she fell to the floor.

Dow rushed to her side, feeling helpless, as what to do for her. He picked her up tenderly and carried her to the bed. He ran for cool water over a cloth and placed on her head to revive her. This was the extent of his nursing skills. The coolness of the water on the back of her neck and forehead brought Anna back to consciousness, only to feel stabbing pains piercing her abdomen. She whispered to Dow in such a faint voice that he had to bend low to hear, "the baby's coming, and its two months too soon."

Hannah, hearing the commotion, came into the room. Dow

was excited trying to tell her what had happened. "She's having the baby too soon." Hannah, still only speaking and understanding German, had to appeal to Anna, "I'm having the baby too soon Mama." To Dow she ordered, "Get Nellie next door to come to me, and then go for the doctor." Dow was out the door and on his way like the hounds of hell was after him.

Nellie entered the house and rushed up the stairs, finding Anna in her bed. Hannah had helped her to get into a nightgown. "I'm here Anna, for whatever help I can be. I'm sure the doctor will get here soon." Anna smiled at her weakly, "thank you Nellie, I'm glad you're here." Anna was in a great deal of pain. Nellie drew up a chair, prepared to settle in for a long night, and hoped for the doctor to arrive before things got so bad she couldn't handle it. Normal childbirth was enough to bear as it was, but this was premature childbirth, and there was no telling how it might end up. Sometimes the baby would die, and sometimes the mother would as well.

Dr. Taylor had a home and office on North Tenth-Street, so Dow was able to reach him in a short time, but still it seemed like an eternity to get him back to Anna. The doctor announced that nothing could be done but let nature take it's course. At last, just before sun up, a very tired and exhausted Anna pushed a tiny frail baby boy into the world. He was so feeble, only a little kittenish mew came instead of a robust cry. Doctor Taylor shook his head, "he must only weigh three pounds, if that. It will be a miracle if he survives." Anna never heard any of this; she had sunken into the oblivion of sound sleep when the pain was over.

The chirping of early birds announced that a new day was dawning. Doctor Taylor walked out to his buggy, his patient horse, ready to take him home and be unhitched with a hearty breakfast of oats in his feed box.

Nellie bustled about the kitchen helping Hannah to put together a good breakfast for Dow and the children, who would be awake soon. They would be excited to learn that the doctor had been there during the night and brought them a new baby brother in his black leather bag. That is what the children were often told; too bad it couldn't be the truth, instead of the pain, suffering, and anguish poor Anna had gone through that long night.

The first one into the kitchen was eight-year-old Leonard. "Where's Mama?" Nellie replied, "She's not feeling too well this morning, so I'm here to help her. I'm going to fix you a good hot breakfast." Margaret came running into the kitchen upon hearing this, "I can help, I know where things are kept. Mama lets me help lots of times, and we bake lots of cookies." Wayne came in, bringing three year old Fred, who climbed up into the wooden high chair. Nellie served the children and remarked, "If you eat all your breakfast, I'll show you the surprise that came last night." "What's the prize?" Little Fred shouted from his high chair. "Shhh, all in good time," Nellie replied with a wink of her eye.

After they had cleaned their plates, she took Fred from the high chair and motioned for them to follow her into their mother's room. She had made sure Anna was up to it, and had brought her a cup of hot tea. They saw their mother sitting up in bed sipping her tea. In a basket, by the side of the bed, lay a very tiny infant. The children gathered around the basket, each asking questions about the new baby. "Is it a boy baby or a girl baby?" Margaret wanted to know. She was hoping for a sister, since she was outnumbered by boys. Anna knew she would be disappointed with her answer, "It's a little boy, and we've named him Virling after a close friend of your Papa's. I'm going to need a lot if help with him. He's very tiny; we must carry him on a pillow when we pick him up."

Leonard went to give his mother a hug before he left the room. Wayne was already out the door with little Fred right behind him. Nellie took Margaret by the hand and led her from the bedside. "Get some rest Anna; I'll be here to look after things until you're up and around again. I'll help your mother with Mr. Waking too. She's tired out after last night, so I sent her to rest." "Bless you Nellie," Anna replied. "What would I have done without you?" Nellie stopped at the door and answered, "You've helped so many others in their time of need, and it's time you got some help in return."

In time, Anna was back in charge of her family and the household. Virling required a lot of special care, but he had survived. If his progress was slower than she remembered, from her other children, she really didn't have the time in her busy schedule to pay it much attention. As the months passed, she came to realize that Virling, being premature as he had been, would never catch up to where he should be. He would always be a little slower to walk, talk, and do things for himself.

CHAPTER 10

THE PASSING OF FRED WAKING

On a beautiful autumn day, with the leaves changing and briskness into the air, Anna went out to her garden, to prepare it for the winter. Each day, she added a task to her daily routine, in order to get her fall house cleaning done. Blankets and quilts that had been put away in cedar chests, were brought out and aired on the clothesline, in preparation for cold nights. Fireplaces were readied for fires and chimneys inspected for bird nests that could stop up the flue.

Anna had the house spic-and-span, ready for the holiday season. Thanksgiving with all the family gathered together, and the joyous Christmas with all the traditions in the big family home on Tenth-Street. Anna stood at the front window and looked out at the snow, softly falling, just as she had many Christmas's ago.

The weather was cold and the ground covered with snow. February was a dreary month. Anna thought it was just as dreary indoors, her Papa was worse than ever. He had been fighting his battle with cancer for several years. Anna was doing all she could to make him comfortable and happy. He wanted his granddaughters to be baptized at his bedside. Anna arranged the baptism, making Margaret, Marjorie, and Myrtle new dresses for the occasion. How glad she was that she had fulfilled his last request, for a few days later her Papa passed away.

A crepe was placed on the front door of the Waking home. The house was put in mourning. All the shades were drawn, the shutters closed, and the women dressed in black. The funeral took place in the front parlor of the house, with the Pastor of St. Paul's Church to officiate.

Anna watched, as her Papas casket was carried out to the hearse. It was all draped in black, with glass sides to enable the casket to be viewed inside. Black horses pulled it to the Lutheran Cemetery. Hannah, with Anna, Dow, and their children followed behind in their buggy, with the rest of the family and friends following, in a horse and buggy procession.

At the graveside, Anna took a rose, again thinking of the words of her favorite hymn, "I come to the garden alone, while the dew is still on the roses, and He walks with me, and He talks with me, and He tells me I am his own." She placed the last rose on the casket, "Go with God Papa, no more pain for you to suffer, but so much pain for us to lose you." Dow placed his arm around her to lead her away from the graveside and back to the buggy. A gust of cold frigid air caused her to pull the fur scarf up closer around her neck, and she thought back to that happy Christmas when her Papa had given it to her and she started to cry again. The tears blurring her sight as she stumbled to the waiting buggy.

The following weeks were hard for Anna to get through, trying to handle her feelings of loss, and concern for her Mama. Hannah finally opened the shutters again. She went to their room. Fred had kept his clothes in a long box at the foot of the bed.

Hannah opened the box and took out all of his clothes. One piece at a time, she placed them all back in the box again and closed it. She left the room and closed and locked the door. That room was never opened again.

CHAPTER 11

TRAGEDY

The cold weather finally past and the warm spring rain had come to sprout new life into the flowers and trees. Dow entered the kitchen, where Anna was peeling potatoes for a part of their evening meal. "I've got something for you, from an old friend. They're on the porch, come and see." Anna put aside her pan of potatoes and started for the front of the house. When she opened the door, she saw them, two of the most beautiful rose bushes she had ever seen. "Where did they come from? What old friend?" she asked. Dow grinned proud to be a part of it all. "Well, it happens, I was on a plumbing job out at Hills, and Joe asked me how you were doing since your Dad passed away. He brought out these rose bushes and asked me to bring them to you." Anna wiped away a tear, "They are so beautiful, I'll plant them in a special place in my rose garden, and I will send him a thank you note for them tomorrow."

Anna had always tended a garden; she loved flowers and especially roses. She felt close to God as she knelt and planted the seeds or little plantings of flowers, vegetables, or herbs. Even in town, her kitchen garden produced tomatoes, peppers, onions, and lettuce. To season in her kitchen, she grew herbs, such as sage, basil, and even peppermint. She loved to experiment with new recipes, and added a special touch to each dish, making it more attractive when serving. She wanted it to look good as well as taste good. To Anna, if anything was worth doing, it was worth doing well.

It was a lovely warm June afternoon. Anna could hear the children playing in the back yard. The house was quiet except for the sounds of the treadle sewing machine. Anna was making Margaret a new dress. Anna loved to sew and was so absorbed in her task of pushing the material under the needle of the machine that she didn't hear the sound of the screen door as it was opened and closed.

It startled her when her brother Bill called her name, "Anna!" She called back to him, "I'm in here sewing." He came into the room, "Anna, come away from the machine, I have something to tell you." She looked at his stricken face and she knew it was not going to be pleasant. She left the sewing machine and took his hand. He led her to the sofa and sat beside her. Tears ran down his face as he told her, "Fred was killed at his job on the railroad today." Anna was stunned, his words repeating inside her head. Her darling brother Fred killed! It cannot be! She was remembering his visit just last Sunday with Edith and how happy they were; since they had adopted the little girl they had named Myrtle. "Does Edith know?" Anna asked. "Yes," Bill replied, she was notified right away. One of the men from the railroad came by the shop to tell me, so I could come and try to make it a bit easier on the family. The railroad men are feeling bad about this. It was all a bad mistake." Bill put his hands over his eyes, preferring not to say anything more, but he knew Anna was going to ask.

She would want to know everything, no matter how much it was going to hurt. "How did it happen?" Anna was starting to cry; the impact of his words had just registered. Bill reached down, took both of her hands, and held them. He took a deep breath to steady his voice so he could answer her. "They were working on a railroad bridge. A train was coming and the foreman insisted they drive one more stake. The train was getting too close, so the other workers dove into the water below, but Fred tried to run to the other side and he didn't make it. The train killed him instantly." Anna collapsed into his arms and sobbed. Dow entered the room, he had closed the plumbing shop to come home and help Anna as best as he could through her sorrow. All he could do was hold her. He wasn't good with words and words mean nothing to anyone at a time like this. She cried until she was exhausted and there were no tears left.

Dow tried to get Anna to go to their room and rest, but to no avail. "I must go to Mama. Bill will have told her by now and she will need me, besides there's Edith, I must go to her." "Edith and Myrtle are coming here as soon as they get a few things together. They have been sent for. Mary and Caroline will be here soon also," Dow informed her. Soon the house was a blur of activity. Friends, neighbors, and family from near and far came to help. Food was brought in and meals prepared.

Anna looked at the crepe on the front door, with its big black satin bow, which brought back memories of death that had visited that house before. Once, when she was a little girl, her four year old brother died from lung fever. She hadn't understood death then, the Pastor had said something like, "he makeith me to lie down in green pastures." She had looked at the pasture scene painting, on the wall. "So this must be the pasture he speaks of," she thought. "That would be nice, to lie in a pasture of sweet smelling grass."

She understood now, death had come again, only a few months ago, and her beloved Papa was taken from them. Now Fred had been taken from her and she would only have the memories of her blond, blue-eyed, brother that smiled at her across the room, on that special Christmas, Easter morning, and on her wedding day. "God must have needed him for something special," Anna would say to herself and to the others. She had a strong faith and it was well that she had, for her sorrows were not to end.

On the morning of the funeral, she went out to her rose garden and with the dew still on the roses; she picked the best one for Fred. Life goes on, as it must, especially when there are children to care for and prepare to send back to school.

The holidays brought some cheerfulness to the big white house on Tenth-Street. Anna loved Christmas, and she always wanted her family to have the best holiday she could give them. Leonard and Wayne each got a new sled, a doll for Margaret, and a toy fire engine pulled by iron horses for Fred. Dow had made wooden blocks for Virling, which he stacked and toppled over.

As Anna left the church and encountered the frosty air swirling with flakes of snow, she pulled the fur closer about her throat which reminded her of the Christmas her Papa had given it to her and tears welled up in her eyes, making it hard for her to see where she was going. Dow helped her into the buggy and put a protective arm about her. "It's been a tough year; let us hope that the New Year will be a better one."

When spring came with its warm breezes, and the beginning of new life came to the earth, Anna knew she would also be bringing a new life into the world. The doctor said it would be late September. Her health was fine, and she had the energy to do spring cleaning, plant her kitchen garden, and tend to her flowers. Dow tried to help as he could, and urged her to rest more.

There was no anxiety about a recurrence like Virling's birth. She had become resigned to the fact that he was a slow child and would always be so. He was quiet and shy, rarely showed a temper, but when he did, it was a tempest, with him throwing himself to the floor and banging his head. It is well we cannot see into the future. Anna had well behaved children. Nothing could have prepared her for the little tempestuous tornado that would enter her life next.

Anna was clearing the dishes from the dining room table. It was early August and she was sticky with the heat. She moved slowly, her body heavy with child and thought, "next month, even if it's late in the month, this will all be over. I'm hot, tired, and as soon as I get the kitchen cleaned up, I'm going to sit out on the porch."

Hannah was still sitting at her place at the table. She couldn't stand long on her swollen legs. "You still fixed a good supper Anna. The tomatoes fresh, are right out of your garden, and the lettuce too. What did you add to the pork chops that made them so good?" "A very simple little trick Mama," replied Anna. "It's just a very light sprinkle of cinnamon."

Leonard came running into the room, "Uncle Matt is here, he wants to see Papa." "Your Papa is out by the grape arbor," She told him, while untying her apron, and went to see her brother-in-law. Matt had helped himself to a chair in the parlor. He arose when Anna entered the room. "Hello Matt, I see Myrtle didn't come with you." She took her usual chair, and he reseated himself." "Not this time," he replied. He was glad to see Dow had entered the room. They shook hands and he said to him, "I've come to bring you bad news, Mama died a little while ago. I came on over here as soon as I could."

Dow was stunned, "what happened to her?" "It was her heart,"

Matt answered. "She went fast before anyone could do a thing." Anna thought, "Poor Dow, it's always been my family, this is his first time to deal with death." Matt arose to leave and Dow followed him to the porch continuing their conversation.

Anna went back to the kitchen and found Margaret working over the dishpan, and Hannah helping with drying. "That's a good girl Margaret, you're getting to be a big help around here, and I certainly need it right now. Your Grandma Boswell has passed away, and I need to spend some time with your Papa now." To Hannah she remarked, "I can't even go to the funeral, I'm too close to my time and Whitewater is too far away. I'm sure they will understand that." She found Dow sitting on the porch, and she joined him to give him what comfort she could.

CHAPTER 12

MARGARET TAKES A STAND

Eight-year-old Margaret entered the kitchen as she did every morning for her breakfast before leaving for school. This morning her Grandmother Hannah was in the kitchen instead of her mother. A strange looking, black coat, was draped over a kitchen chair. She thought her Grandmother seemed to be in a hurry to hustle her out the door. She handed her a head scarf and said goodbye to her in German as she waved her out the door.

Margaret had almost reached school, when she discovered she didn't have her schoolbook. She had been hustled out so fast she had forgotten it. As she rushed back home to get her book, she pushed open the kitchen door and heard a baby cry. Her Grandmother sat on a kitchen chair with a tiny red, squalling baby across her lap. "I forgot my book. Where did that come from?" she asked, trying to catch her breath from rushing. Hannah lifted the baby now wrapped in a pink blanket and said to her, "This is your new baby sister Dortkin." "That is the ugliest baby, I ever saw," shouted Margaret and she turned on her heel and ran out of the house and back to school.

Anna and Dow had named their new daughter Dorothy May, but Leonard hearing his Grandmother call her name in German, as Dortkin, laughed and called her that many times over the years to come to tease her.

The new baby required a great deal of Anna's attention. She didn't get to church herself, but she ensured that the children were dressed and ready every Sunday. Margaret had a new coat with plaid collar and cuffs, and a tam o' shanter hat to match. She hadn't told her mother that her cousins, Jesse and Farrel, had been teasing her every Sunday as she walked to church. Aunt Iowa's house was at the corner of South Ninth and A Street, so they made sure to catch up to her on Seventh Street, almost to the church. Margaret would see them waiting for her about a block from the church, and they would start pointing at her and laughing. Jesse yelled out, "Here comes Piggy, and she's got a big flat pancake on her head! Where did you get that stupid pancake hat Piggy?" Margaret stopped, turned her back, and retraced her steps going back the way she came, until she stood in front of St. Johns Lutheran Church at the corner of Seventh and South E. Street. She watched the congregation entering and she followed. She had made up her mind; she would not go to St. Paul's anymore.

Week after week went by and the family never knew of her decision, until Mrs. Schultz stopped by for a visit with Anna to see how the new baby was doing. Anna was always glad to have company, and Mrs. Schultz was a favorite. Anna made tea and showed off her new daughter, Dorothy, proudly. Dorothy was on her best behavior and cooed nicely for the company. Virling sat under the dining room table stacking his blocks. He didn't talk to company at all. Mrs. Shultz knew all the latest gossip in the neighborhood, and was happy to share it with Anna. As they sipped their tea, the subject was brought up concerning St.

Paul's church. Mrs. Schultz said, "That reminds me, I wanted to ask you about Margaret, I haven't seen her at church for several weeks. "Haven't you?" Anna asked. "Well, I will have to ask her not to keep to herself so much." She was not about to let Mrs. Shultz know that this was news to her, because she saw her go off to church every Sunday. Anna quickly thought and changed the subject abruptly by showing her the rose that was contained in a bud vase on a nearby table. "What do you think of this? My last rose, for the summer that bloomed late in the year. I really hate to see winter come because I miss working among my flowers." Mrs. Schultz, rising from her chair, said, "I really must be going now, but I've got to say I don't know how you manage to get so much done around here with six children to care for and keep your lovely garden too. Everything is always just perfect."

St. Paul's Lutheran Church

Anna was waiting for Margaret, when she came through the door from school. "Margaret, come and sit down, I want to talk to you. Have you been going to church?" "Yes, Mama," Margaret replied, "but not to St. Paul's. I've been going to St. John's. I like it better there." "Did something happen at St. Paul's that you don't like?" Anna wanted to know. Margaret then decided to tell her mother about Jesse and Farrel. Anna was mad, but she didn't want Margaret to see how upset this had made her, so she patted her arm and told her to continue going to St. John's if she liked.

She hadn't seen much of Dow's family of late. Iowa and Clayton would stop by for a short visit now and then, but it had been awhile. Mag didn't come into town very often, and Flo had returned to Mississippi after her mother's funeral. She decided she wouldn't mention this to Dow. His nieces being mean to his daughter would not sit well with him.

"Anna, I just got a new job," Dow informed his wife as he entered the kitchen." Henry offered me a job at the Starr Piano Factory, and I took it. This means a new start for us and a home of our own. There's a big house over on Charles-Avenue I can rent. I'd like to take you over there to see if it suits." "Right now?" Anna asked, excited at the prospect of going somewhere, anywhere at all. "Yes, I thought we could go now. I left the buggy hitched." Dow started for the door. "I'll be right there, as soon as I can get this apron off, and get my hat, scarf, and gloves."

Anna hurried up the stairs, looked in the nursery to see if Dorothy was still sleeping. Five year old Virling was playing on the floor at his grandmother's feet while she sat in her big chair shelling peas. "I'll be out for awhile Mama, but I'll be back before the children get home from school." Hannah nodded and smiled up at her, she could see Anna was excited about going somewhere. "Go along and enjoy your afternoon."

The afternoon was perfect for a drive. The horses went at a clip clop up Tenth-Street to Main Street, and turned west going down Main-Street and across the Main-Street Bridge. When they reached Charles-Avenue, Dow pulled the reins and the horses stopped in front of a large, white, two story house, with a porch across the front and down the side, with the front entrance at the side porch. An iron fence with a gate enclosed the yard.

Dow helped Anna from the buggy and opened the gate. Two wide steps led to the porch. Dow took a key from his pocket and unlocked the door. Stepping inside the vacant house, she saw the possibilities it offered as a comfortable home. The rooms were large with high ceilings. A stair case in the hall, led to numerous rooms upstairs, another smaller stairway in the hall upstairs led to attic rooms. One room in the front gable facing the street had three decorative windows. Anna also made a tour of the yard, noting the garden that was there and spots where other gardens could be placed. "I think this will do nicely, plenty of room for six lively children." The family settled well into the house on Charles-Avenue. Leonard celebrated his Thirteenth birthday, Wayne following with his Twelfth, and Margaret her Tenth. Eight year old Fred attended school with them, leaving Anna in a quiet house with five year old Virling and baby Dorothy. Her early morning sickness told her that before this year was out, she would be having another, to add to the household. Dr. Bond confirmed it, setting the date for early September.

That evening, at the dinner table, she told the family the news of a new baby in the fall. It was always the custom that each, in turn, tell about their day. This evening Dow said he had a story to tell. "I went to the bank to cash my check today. The teller counted it out so fast; I decided I had better count it again. I was right outside the door on Main-Street. She gave me ten dollars too much, so I went right back into the bank and told her she had made a mistake. She asked me "Were you outside the bank?" I told her "yes", and before I could say another word, she said to me quite sassy, "After you leave the bank we don't rectify mistakes." and she slammed the cage door so fast she almost caught my fingers." Anna asked him "What will you do about it?" "Tomorrow I'll go back to the bank and see if her attitude has changed, since by now she must know she came up ten dollars short. If she's still snippy, well, then she just made a donation to St. Paul's Lutheran Church!"

On September Tenth, 1913, Anna gave birth to a beautiful baby boy. They named him Roland Dow. He was a good baby, and easy to care for. Dorothy, on the other hand was going into her terrible two's, and giving more trouble than all of the children put together. Dow spoiled her terribly, and Anna told him he was making a mistake not to discipline her when she was naughty.

Children

CHAPTER 13

CHRISTMAS OF 1915

Christmas of 1915, Anna decided it would be special. Everything was going well, and she wasn't pregnant. She went shopping to get everyone a special gift. Leonard was fifteen now and wanted a suede jacket, Wayne wanted a watch, and Margaret wanted a doll. She was twelve years old and too old for baby dolls, but this one was special with a real china head and bridal attire. Fred was getting a sled, Virling a tent he could crawl into, and Dorothy a little rocking chair. Roland was two now and a little horse on wheels would be just right for him.

Dow brought in a fresh tree he had cut on Clayton Hunt's farm, and they set it up in front of the parlor window. Anna brought down the decorations from the attic, and they all joined in, to place the garlands of tinsel, and the ornaments, they all remembered from year to year. Small tin candleholders were attached to the branches. The candles would be lit for a short time on Christmas Eve, and again on Christmas morning. They had to be watched closely for fear of catching the tree on fire. There were special treats to enjoy, popcorn balls, a big bowl of oranges, tangerines, apples, and dishes of hard candies, and fudge.

The family gathered around the tree to open their gifts, besides their special ones, there were others. Leonard, Wayne and Margaret each got a bank to save their money. One was a bear, another one, a dog, and an elephant. Margaret was happy to have the doll she had picked out in Woolworth's window. She carried it about all day.

Dorothy had been getting into mischief all day. She got bored with her own gifts, and wanted everybody else's. She took Roland's horse which made him cry. She took over Virling's tent and he was having a tantrum, and finally, she insisted on holding Margaret's doll. Margaret said "No!" Dorothy ran to Papa. "I want to hold it." Dow said, "Let her hold it for a little while." Margaret said, no, she'll break it!" Dow said, "Just for a minute." Margaret handed the doll over to Dorothy. Dorothy took the doll, gave it a look, and deliberately threw it to the floor, breaking the beautiful china head into bits and pieces. Margaret screamed, "I knew it! I told you she would break it." and she left the room crying, and flew up the stairway to her room to cry her heart out.

Anna was disgusted with Dorothy, and even more so with Dow for insisting that Margaret gives up her doll. Now she looked at him, waiting to see if he decided to punish her, but he just picked up the fragments of the doll and left the room. Christmas was spoiled now, and Anna was angry. "Are you happy now Missy?" You go tell your Papa to put you to bed, I'm going up to see your sister and when I come down, I had better not find you still here or it won't be pleasant!"

Anna went up the stairs to Margaret's room and tapped lightly on the door. She entered and took Margaret into her arms. She kissed Margaret's tear stained face. "I'm so sorry, this has ruined your Christmas and mine also." She then went to her room, not bothering to go back downstairs. Every one of the children had left for their own rooms when they saw what Dorothy had done. Fred had taken little Roland with him.

When Dow came into the room, she asked, "What are we going to do about that child? She needs to be disciplined, as I told you before. She's getting out of hand." Dow shook his head, "I've never whipped a child, or an animal. I don't know what to do with her. We've never had a child as willful as she is. Maybe she'll grow out of it." Anna remarked as she got into bed, "I doubt it!"

CHAPTER 14

TRAGEDY STRIKES AGAIN

In April 1916, Anna found that she was again going to have another baby. She had just turned forty in March. "I'm getting too old for this, I'm not as spry as I used to be," she told Dow. She managed the household as she always had, worked her vegetable garden and her flowers. Roland followed her everywhere from house to garden. The summer garden supplied the family with plenty of fresh food, and Anna canned fruits and vegetables for the winter. Leonard and Wayne picked the cherries from the trees at their Grandmother's house on Tenth Street and Anna made pies and canned the rest for winter.

It was early November, when Anna was sadly told the news, that her brother Bill had been killed. She had always been so proud of him. He had taken over the family business and was doing so well. He was one of the few to own an automobile, and was on a business trip for the plumbing company, when his automobile was struck by a train at a main crossing in Liberty, Indiana. The automobile had been demolished and carried almost a block before the train could be stopped. The train had given no warning, as witnessed by people that had seen the accident. He was so badly injured, that he couldn't survive.

Anna put on her mourning clothes once again, and set out to her mother's and then to her sister-in-law's house. Mollie went to Dow as soon as they arrived. "I've got a big favor to ask of you, I need you to come back to the plumbing shop. I can't handle this alone. There's a big plumbing contract for Easthaven that must be completed." "I'll start as soon as I can," Dow replied. Bill's widow Mollie was so appreciative for all his help, in coming back to the business, that she gave each of the boys a new bicycle from the shop for Christmas. Four days after Christmas, Anna presented them with a new baby brother. They christened him Lorenzo Dow. "I want him named after you," she told her husband, "for surely this is the last."

Margaret was fourteen and decided she was a young lady, and wanted to distance herself from the family, mainly from Dorothy, because she never forgot the doll incident. One morning she approached her mother about her plan, "Mama, would it be alright if I moved up into the attic room?" Anna thought a moment and answered her, "yes, if you can do it by yourself, I can't huff and puff up another flight of stairs." Margaret went for cleaning supplies and began making the attic room her own. First she washed the three ornate windows that fronted on Charles-Avenue. Then she opened them and let the early summer air into the spacious room. She swept and mopped the wide wooden boards of the floor, and wiped the walls and woodwork of dust and cobwebs. Now for the furnishings, she went to see the whereabouts of Leonard and Wayne, for help in moving her bed to the upper floor. Each of them was in a wicker rocking chair on the front porch. "I'm moving up to the attic, will you help me get my bed up there?" she asked. "Yeah, I'll help." Leonard replied, and

Wayne just got up to follow them. When they reached the upper room and saw how nice it looked, Wayne said, "Gee, I wish I had thought of this. It's nice up here." They worked and struggled to get the bed and feather mattress up the steps, and set it up again close to the windows. "Gees, that was good of you fellows to help me out." "That's okay Sis, but we can't get that heavy bureau up here," Leonard told her. Margaret shook her head, "I know, I'll find something else to sit things on."

After they left the room, she started to rummage. Opening a door that led to a back attic, dark with no windows, she thought she saw something she could use. As her eyes became accustomed to the dimness, she made out to be, what had once been used as a wash stand. It was made of Oak, and had a drawer and a bottom compartment that opened. She opened the door of the compartment to find an old fashioned Pitcher and Washbowl in blue and white flowered porcelain. She was excited at her find. "I can use this," she said to herself.

She took them to her new room, and went back to pull and wiggle the washstand to her room also. She wiped it down to get rid of the dust and grime. It looked as if it might have had a mirror attached to it at one time, and it had a towel rack at the side. At last, she brought a small rocking chair from her old room, her personal belongings, and went to tell her mother, "I'm moved in!"

Little Lorenzo was a delight and a beautiful child. "He is perfect in every way," Anna said. Even Dorothy loved him and was very protective of him. All of the children went to school except baby Lorenzo, Roland, and Dorothy. Virling even was enrolled in a special class. "It's time to send Dorothy to school this year," said Anna. "I've made her some new dresses and got her a lunch pail, so tomorrow before you leave for work, walk her to school and enroll her."

They told Dorothy of their plan, but she didn't like it. Anna had her up early, and dressed in a new dress, with her hair combed back and tied with a big bow. While Dorothy ate her breakfast, with a towel covering her dress, Anna packed her lunch pail. "I put in a special treat for first day," Anna informed her. Dow took Dorothy by the hand and they set out, across the field, behind the house for Easthaven Avenue School.

Anna had just finished washing the breakfast dishes, and she happened to look out the kitchen window, when she saw Dorothy coming across the field as fast as she could run. Anna met her at the door, "what did you do?" "I ran away," laughed Dorothy. "Well, Missy, tomorrow you will go back," said Anna. The next day, she was prepared for school, and Dow again walked her to school and waited until she was seated, and class had begun, before he left for work. Anna had gotten the first load of wash out to the clothesline, in the backyard, and when she looked up from the basket, here again, was Dorothy coming across the field. "How did you leave school?" Dorothy again, laughing at her trick said, "I raised my hand to go to the out house, and then I just came on home." "This is going to stop, I'll take you to school tomorrow," said Anna.

When Anna took Dorothy to school the next day, she spoke to the teacher. "Miss Pentecost, we must find a way to stop this running away from school." I can handle her, but I need your permission to spank her if necessary, said the teacher." "It will kill my soul to have it done, but do it if you must," replied Anna. After she returned home, Anna watched the field all day for signs of Dorothy, but this time she stayed at school.

When the school day was over and Dorothy came home she seemed happy. Anna questioned her about her day, "Did you try to leave school today?" "Yes," Dorothy replied. "I tried, but she caught me, and then she put me across her knees, and she spanked my butt. Then she pulled up a chair for me, to sit beside her desk and gave me a pretty picture book to look at. I just love her!"

Dorothy's time at school was cut short after all one day, when the teacher sent her home. She was crying as she entered the house. "What's the matter? Why are you home so early?" Anna wanted to know. "I got sick at school. I don't feel good. Teacher sent me home," Dorothy cried. Anna felt her forehead, she was burning with fever. "Let's get you into bed right away, and as soon as the boys get home they can get the Doctor."

Leonard arrived home first, and at first glance at him, she knew he was sick also. His face was flushed, and his eyes looked glassy. "Are you sick too?" She asked him. He just nodded, and went to his room, anxious to lie down. Virling arrived home next, and she was thankful to see he was fine. Wayne had waited to walk home with Fred. Anna greeted them at the door. "How do you feel?" Leonard and Dorothy are both sick. "We're okay, but lots of kids are out of school sick," Fred answered. Margaret arrived home later than usual, stopping by a friend's house on the way. Her Papa was just leaving the house to get the doctor. "Go help your Mama, Leonard and Dorothy have come down with something, I've got to get the doctor right away."

When Dr. Taylor arrived, he examined Dorothy first. He just shook his head and said, "Another case of it, she's got diphtheria, it's all over town. Let's take a look at your son." On the examination of Leonard, the diagnosis was the same. He left some medicine, and put a yellow Quarantine sign by the front door. "No one leaves this house, or comes in," he said. He also said he would be back to check on the rest of the family in a few days. Dow couldn't go to work, and as it turned out, he was needed more at home. Wayne had come down with the illness, and so did Fred. Even though Roland was kept away from the sick rooms, he caught it as well, and he had it worse than the rest.

Anna from the first night, when she found out what the sickness was, had gone to Margaret. "I need you to help me. I want you to take the baby to your upstairs room and don't come down. I will wash and change my clothes before I bring a tray of food for you and him. Leave your soiled clothes, and his, in the bathroom, but wear a mask when you come out of your room to go. I'll bring fresh diapers and leave them in a basket outside your door. Who would have thought when you took the attic room, how much we would need it to keep the baby as far away from the sickness as we can."

Anna was worn out, but there was no rest. Dow was doing things he had never thought he would. He was hanging out the wash every day, and it was a good thing the weather was sunny and bright to dry them. There were sheets, towels, and nightgowns, not to mention diapers that were in demand constantly. Anna stewed chickens and beef for the broth to feed the sick, for their throats were so sore, a little of the broth was all they could get down.

Thank goodness for all the help they got from the milkman and iceman who left them what they needed and couldn't pay them for at the time. The money, they felt would be contaminated. Clayton brought baskets of food from his store. Anna didn't have time to bake bread now. She barely had time for more than a cup of coffee or tea. She was worried about Roland. She sat with him night and day, as much as she could, and still tend to the rest. He had gone from a robust little boy down to a thin frail little being. She hated to be from his side for a minute. From early morning to late at night she went from room to room changing beds, washing off hot little bodies, trying to get a bit of broth into them to keep them alive. She raised them up and supported them when the coughing spasms were at their worst.

As the days passed, it began to look as if the sickness was losing its grip on them, all except for Roland. Anna now sat by his bedside all night. She was afraid he would slip away from her, and one morning at four o'clock he did. Her precious little boy was gone. She continued to sit there with him, tears streaming from her eyes. She knew it was Sunday, she heard St. Andrew's bells ring for seven o'clock mass.

The funeral was private because of the quarantine. The pastor of St. Paul's came to the house the following afternoon, at three o'clock, for the services. They buried him next to his Grandfather Waking at the Lutheran Cemetery. Every Sunday from then on Anna made a visit to the cemetery to place flowers on his grave. She had mourned when she lost her father and brothers, but there was no loss like losing your child.

Easthaven State Hospital

CHAPTER 15

DOW'S JOB THE STATE
HOSPITAL FOR THE INSANE

The crisp cool days of autumn had passed, and winter was coming on. Anna got through each day as she must. The family was well again and back to school. The house was quiet with just baby Lorenzo, and she said, "he was always good as gold." It was time to be thinking of Christmas preparations, and for Lorenzo's first birthday. She hated the thought of Christmas without Roland. "I must get myself together; the children and Dow will be counting on me."

Anna heard the back door open, and she went to see who this was home early. She screamed when she saw Dow standing there. His clothes were torn to shreds, his face and arms bloody with long scratches. "What happened to you Dow?" He got to a kitchen chair and sank down onto it before he answered. "It was a patient at Easthaven that done this. I was installing a new sink at the women's section; no one was supposed to be in there. They usually have a guard to make sure, I don't know where she was. The door flew open and there she was, a big woman with her hair sticking out wildly all over her head. She yelled when she saw me, and then she came at me, grabbed my shirt sleeve and tore it, and raked my arm with her fingernails. I tried to get away from her. By the time two matrons got her down and gave her a needle in her arm, I was all torn up."

Anna got him a cup of coffee, and filled a basin with hot water. She removed his shirt, or what was left of it, and started to wash his wounds. "You're not going back there. I must get some iodine to put on these scratches, they could get infected." He winced as she applied the medication. "I don't want to go back there. I always felt bad to be where the windows have heavy wire over them, but I guess I never thought it was dangerous."

That night at the dinner table, the children wanted to know why he was painted up like an Indian on the warpath. "I got into a skirmish with a wild woman who got out of her cage. Say, did I ever tell you about the time the Indians found me under the bed when I was a little boy out on the prairie in Iowa?" "Yes!" they all shouted.

Dorothy wanted to tell her story, of what had happened at school that day, so she started in, only to be interrupted by Wayne. "Mama, can't you sit her somewhere else at the table? She eats all those onions and then it's "she said," and "he said," and breathing her onion breath all over me!" Anna laughed for the first time in a long time. "I thought by placing her between you and Leonard that you could handle her."

CHAPTER 16

HANNA'S ILLNESS

It was early spring, and Anna was glad to be out in her garden among her flowers. She was setting out a new rose bush that she was eager to see bloom. Margaret came out to the garden to remind her, "it's time to leave for the Circus Parade." Leonard, Wayne and Fred had already left for the Circus grounds; they hoped they might earn their tickets to the Big top by carrying water to the animals.

Anna, with Margaret and the younger children, walked to the car line and rode the interurban as far as Tenth and Main Streets. Anna's intention was for her mother to walk up to Main-Street and join them to see the parade. "Margaret, run down to Grandma's and bring her for the parade."

Margaret ran as fast as she could, because she didn't want to miss anything. When she rapped at the door there was no answer, so she tried the door and finding it unlocked, she opened it and entered the quiet house. "Grandma, its Margot." she called. A faint answer came from her Grandma's bedroom. Upon entering the room, Margaret saw that she was very ill. "I'm going to get Mama and some help for you right away."

Margaret ran even faster this time to reach her Mama. "Mama, come quick, I think Grandma's dying!" Anna sent her back along with Virling and Dorothy, and she entered a nearby store and called for an ambulance. She then started down Tenth-Street herself carrying Lorenzo. She arrived shortly before the ambulance arrived. She sat down by the bed and took Hannah's hand. "I've called for an ambulance, and it will be here soon to take you to the hospital. They will take good care of you, and I will be there as soon as I can." Margaret had led the ambulance helpers to her Grandma's room and watched as they put her on a stretcher and carried her to the waiting ambulance. Anna watched as the vehicle sped away with its siren blaring.

"Come children, I must lock up here and then get you home so I can get to the hospital." By the time they had reached Main-Street, the end of the Circus parade was passing. "I'm sorry you missed it," she told them. "Sometimes things don't go as you plan."

Anna was informed that her Mother was not going to get better. Arrangements were made for Hannah to make her home with them, on Charles-Avenue, when she left the hospital. Anna would take care of her, as Hannah had always taken care of her. Anna left Margaret to see after baby Lorenzo and her Grandmother, since she was home from school with a monthly headache and cramps. Anna had to go back to the house on Tenth-Street to pack her Mother's things. She walked from room to room remembering the days lived there. She climbed the stairs and entered her room, the room of her girlhood and later shared with Dow. She moved to the window and pushed back the lace curtain, and looked down to Tenth-Street. It was shady and quiet this time of the afternoon. She had stood like this the morning of her wedding, took refuge here when her Papa and brother Fred had died. Virling and Dorothy had been born in this room. She felt a part of her would always be in this room. She took one last look around the room, closed the shutters, and went out the door. She packed the cases and left them by the front door to be picked up later. Before locking the door, she went out to the garden with kitchen shears and a damp tea towel. She cut the stems of the roses and laid each one carefully on the damp towel. She sank to her knees and wept bitterly. Her tear drops falling onto the fresh petals of the roses. When Anna left the house, she decided to change her route, and walk back down South E. Street as she had as a girl going to St. Paul's. She crossed over Seventh, giving a glance up the street to the church and walked past the park. When she reached South Fifth-Street, she turned to go back up to Main-Street and catch the interurban cars.

St. Andrews Catholic Church

She was in front of St. Andrew's Catholic Church when the thought occurred to her, to go in and rest a moment. She knew the doors were always open for anyone to enter and pray at anytime. She hadn't been there since she was a young girl and went inside, out of curiosity. It was cool and dim inside, with a faint odor of incense still in the air. The white gothic spires of the alters gleamed in the light, coming from the large, ornate, stained glass windows that lined both sides of the church depicting Jesus' life.

She chose a pew a short distance down, on the right side, of the main aisle, she genuflected and sat down. There were kneeling benches, but she wasn't ready for that yet. It was so beautiful and quiet and restful. She knew this had been what she was in need of, time to herself, to restore her faith, and it was sorely in need of restoration. She had been through a time she could not describe, with the loss of Roland.

She heard the rustle of heavy material, and looked over to see a priest, dressed in his black cassock, sat down beside her. He asked in a soft voice, "Can I be of help to you today?" She said, "Yes Father you can, I'm in deep mourning for my little son. He was just four years old. He died last fall and I feel so lost, and I don't know why he was taken from me so soon. My mother is ill and I know I will lose her soon as well, but she is ready to be out of pain, and I understand that for her, death will be a blessing. I can get past that; even though, I am going to miss her so very much. She has always been there to help me through the bad times." The Priest nodded and spoke, "there is a purpose to everything in life. We don't always understand what God has in store for us. We must know that God had a purpose for calling him home at that time." He pointed to the roses she held in her hands. "Think of it this way, he was budded on earth to bloom in heaven." He patted her arm and left.

When Anna left the church and walked out into the warm sunlight. She threw her shoulders back and straightened herself. "I've got to be strong, and I will be strong," she promised herself.

Her strength was tested when her mother passed away a few weeks later. A death is a shock, even when it's expected from months of decline, such as Hannah's had been. Anna was relieved that her mother's suffering had come to an end, but she was going to miss her so terribly. It was another funeral to get through and lay her mother to rest next to her father, in Lutherania.

CHAPTER 17

A DAY IN TOWN

Anna was preparing for a day in town, with Margaret at home to over see Lorenzo. Dow was driving the horse and buggy to the plumbing shop, so she could ride along with him. She arranged her hat at the proper angle, adjusted her neck scarf, pulled on her gloves and buttoned them, picked up her pocket book and was out the door. Dow helped her into the buggy and asked, "Do you have your shopping list?" "Yes," she replied, "I have everything." She didn't want to tell him that she also had an appointment at Dr. Taylor's office, that afternoon.

"It's a lovely day, I hope it stays nice and doesn't rain," said Anna. Dow laughed remembering a story he had heard and wanted to tell her. "Speaking of rain, reminds me of a story about this timid young man who asked the livery stable owner about renting a horse and buggy to take his girlfriend for a ride. He told the owner he wasn't familiar with horses, and would want a real gentle horse. The livery owner assured him he had just the right horse for him. He got the young man seated in the open buggy and told him how to use the lap robe, and also where the parasol was located, for his lady-friend to use, if the sun was too hot. Before he drove off, he was again assured the horse was gentle, and the only thing, was to be sure the "rein" didn't get under the horse's tail. After he had been gone awhile, a sudden summer rain storm came up. The young man, with the lady doing the driving, drove into the livery barn while the young man was leaning over, with the open parasol, held over the horse's tail. When asked what he was doing, the young man replied, "You told me not to let the rain get under the horse's tail." Anna started laughing and Dow was pleased to see it. He wanted to bring some joy into her life.

The Livery Stable

Plumbing Shop

Wayne County Courthouse

Dow pulled up to the plumbing shop that was located at 406 Main-Street, across from the courthouse. Anna stepped inside to speak to Mollie. It was difficult to walk with the porcelain footed bathtubs, the latest thing in water closets, and bicycles cluttering the aisles. She found Mollie at the back of the shop, in a tiny office. She looked up seeing Anna, "My goodness, this is a nice surprise. How are you? It's been awhile." "I'm getting along pretty good," Anna answered. "I came into town to do a little shopping, and perhaps we could meet for lunch at the Greek Candy Store." This was agreed upon and Anna started on her way.

St. Hunt's Grocery Store

She stopped at the Hoosier Store at Sixth and Main to buy some yard goods for an apron, and then passing by Hunt's Grocery Store; she encountered Clayton putting a crate of fresh fruit out for display on the sidewalk. "What brings you into town today Anna?" "Oh, I just felt like getting out on such a lovely day and rode in with Dow," she replied. She then hurried on her way, to keep her appointment.

The doctor confirmed that she was pregnant again, and could expect the baby around the first week of February of the coming year. She left his office feeling tired, "I'm getting too old for this," she thought. She went to Knollenberg's Department Store; they had a nice restroom for ladies and a comfortable sitting area at the bottom of the oak staircase leading to the second floor. As usual, she saw someone she knew to sit with and pass the time of day. On this occasion, it was Mrs. Shultz from the neighborhood on Tenth-Street. "I miss your mother so much," she said to Anna. "We also miss you and the youngsters." "I'll always miss Tenth-Street," replied Anna, "that was home." Anna looked at the clock on the wall, "I must be going, I'm meeting Mollie for lunch at the Greek Candy Store, and won't you join us?" Mrs. Shultz said she was expected home, so they left promising to get together soon.

Knollenberg's Department Store

Anna arrived at the Greek Candy Store, at the same time as Mollie, so they entered laughing at their perfect timing. They made their way to the back, of the store, where the ice cream parlor tables and chairs were. The front of the store had glass cases, containing candy of every description, and a long marble soda fountain. The walnut paneled walls were inset with mirrors, and on each mirror the name of one of their soda fountain ice cream confections.

The Greek Candy Store

They ordered chocolate sodas and sandwiches, and enjoyed the treats, while catching up on the family news together. Anna didn't tell her the news about expecting, because Dow must hear that first before anyone else. Even then, it was a secret kept, until it wasn't a secret anymore, from those who saw her. Which were few, since she didn't go about, once it was obvious.

Main Street

They walked back to the plumbing shop, where Dow was waiting to drive her home, checking on a job along their way. He helped her into the buggy, and they set off back across the Main Street Bridge. "I've got something to tell you," began Anna, "I'm going to have another baby. I had an appointment with the doctor today. I wanted to be sure before I said anything. It's for sure, sometime the first week of next February." "How do you feel?" asked Dow. "You thought Lorenzo would be the last one." "Well, I was forty years old when Lorenzo was born; I didn't think there would be anymore. I feel okay, a bit tired out, but I'm no spring chicken anymore." Dow laughed, "I must be a pretty good old rooster though!"

CHAPTER 18

LOTS OF CHANGES

Anna awoke with pain in her back; she knew this was the start of labor. The doctor had said it would be the first week in February and it was February Ninth. It was only a few minutes after midnight. She hated to awaken Dow, but he needed to send for the Doctor. "This is the first birth without Mama," she thought sadly. She snuggled close to Dow and whispered, "Wake up Dow; it's time to go for the doctor." Dow hurriedly dressed and went out into the cold, dark, barn, to hitch up the buggy.

Anna looked at the clock, timing how far apart each pain was. She turned onto her side, to relieve the pain in her back. She would appear to doze off between pains as they tired her. She saw that an hour had passed and she heard a sound in the hall. Dow came into the room and sat down by the bedside. "Doc will be here shortly. How are you doing?" "I think it's getting close," she answered, grimacing with another onslaught of pain. "I guess it's going to be just you and me if the doctor doesn't get here," Anna said to Dow, then moaned with another pain.

Dow started pacing the floor, going to the window to look out into the cold, dark, night, then back to the bedside and looked at the clock ticking away the minutes. Finally he heard a sound on the street and prayed it was the doctor arriving. "I think that's the doctor now Anna, I'll go down and let him in."

He hurried down the stairs, and sure enough he heard steps on the porch. He rushed to open the front door, before the doctor had a chance to knock. He reached out and practically pulled the doctor into the house. Dow gave a big sigh of relief, he had been more afraid than he let on. "I'm glad you're here," he said to the doctor and led the way up the stairs to Anna.

The doctor pulled up a chair next to the bed and opened his black medical bag. He took out his stethoscope to listen to Anna's and the baby's heartbeat. "They're going to be fine," he said to Dow. "I know, I know," Dow said. "I'll go boil some water," and he fled downstairs to the kitchen. When the ordeal was over for Anna, and for Dow, their new baby daughter was presented to them. They were so happy, as if, it had been their first. They looked her all over, counted fingers and toes. "She's perfect Dow and I want to name her after Mama, not Hannah, but the German way it was written, Johanna, and also for mother Kiziah. She will be Kiziah Joann." Dow was all smiles and Anna knew this had made him very happy. This little one was her Papa's pet from then on.

Dow was in the back yard and unaware that a black sedan automobile had parked in front of his house, and two men in suits, carrying, important looking, brief cases had entered his home. Anna had answered the door and led them into the parlor. They gave their names, and the firm they were with, but all that registered with her, was the name Henry Gennett. He was someone her husband was acquainted with, at the Starr Piano Factory.

Home of Henry Gennett

She left them to find Dow, and as she walked back to the house with him, she told him they wanted to question him about Henry. "I won't answer questions about a friend; I'll have nothing to say to them. Follow my lead, and say nothing but yes or no." Upon entering the room, Dow shook hands with each man, in turn, and seated himself in his favorite chair. "What can I do for you gentlemen today?" asked Dow. The tall man in the brown suit seemed to be the leader and asked, "Did you work at the Starr Piano Factory?" Dow assumed a blank look to his face and inquired of Anna, "Anna, was that before or after I went to Easthaven?" A shocked look appeared on the face of the man and he looked at his partner and shook his head. He turned back to Dow, "That will be all, we're sorry to have taken your time." They made their way to the door and Dow watched them drive away with a flurry of hand gestures between them that seemed to signal a futile attempt to get what they were after.

When Dow closed the door laughing, he found Anna looking at him perplexed. "You see Anna, They were looking for someone to testify to something, whatever it was, the mention of me being at Easthaven stopped them cold. My testimony would never hold up. I didn't lie; I never said I was a patient there. I just asked when it was that I was there. You know while I was working there, as a plumber, I was there a lot, more than I liked if fact. Henry is a successful man and there will always be people that want to make a fast buck by trying to sue for it. I don't know if that was the case here, but I never go against a friend, no matter what."

Dow entered the kitchen where Anna was busy preparing their evening meal. "Anna, I've found a new place for us. It's not far away so the schools will be the same. We need a bigger house. Margaret is seventeen now and seems to want to do some entertaining. She's out with friends a lot." The large house was on Southwest Seventh Street across from Earlham College. Anna agreed and the move was made, but the following year, he wanted to move again. This time, they were a bit closer to town. The property, in later years, became the high school football field.

Anna wasn't settled in this house long when he chose a house for them on South Eighteenth-Street. Anna liked this house; it was large and airy with a big shady front porch. She quickly became friends with her neighbors, and her porch became a frequent spot for Judge Hoelscher to stop and visit a while. He always seemed to catch her at a chore of shelling peas or snapping beans. She always liked to be outside in the fresh air as much as she could. He had known her Papa, and the other members of her family. His family had come from Germany as well, and they attended the same church.

On this hot summer afternoon, he was enjoying a glass of

lemonade with chips of ice in it. The ice came from the new oak icebox that Dow had bought, to keep the ice a lot longer. "It sure is refreshing on a hot day like today," he remarked. "I'm glad you're back closer to your old neighborhood." "I hope I can stay, but Mollie is talking of selling the business and moving to Dayton. I know Dow will want to go back to farming. He thinks it would be good for the boys. They're young men now and have odd jobs, but he thinks a farm is the place for them. We may be having a wedding soon. Margaret is keeping company with a fine young man from just north of Richmond. He farms on the Inke Road, belonged to his folks. His name is Joe Tschaen." "I know Joe, he's a fine fellow. He likes automobiles, likes to tinker with motors. Margaret's a good match for him."

The following weekend, Anna tried to remember his words and be heartened by them as she waited up for Margaret to come home. Dow had fallen asleep in his chair, but Anna paced the floor. She walked to the porch and peered up and down the quiet street. She carefully closed the screen door so it wouldn't bang and walked to the kitchen for a drink of water, then back to the parlor. She stopped and looked hard at the mantel clock. It was ticking away the minutes and would soon begin the harsh donging of the midnight hour. This clock had never had a happy chime, but a deep foreboding gong. Just as the clock began its toll, she heard another sound, and there were two very guilty looking faces staring at her. A rush of relief overtook her to be followed by fury. "Where have you been so late?" she asked them with anger in her voice. "I'm sorry to have worried you Mama," began Margaret as Joe approached Dow with his apology as Dow got up from his chair. "Sorry, Sir, we didn't plan to be so long."

Margaret led her mother to the large overstuffed sofa and sat down beside her. "Mama, we're married! I know you have always planned for me to have a church wedding, but I didn't want it. We decided on the spur of the moment and went to a Justice of the Peace." Anna wiped her eyes, "no use crying over spilt milk." That was Margaret for you; she made her decisions and carried them out. Never a thought for tomorrow, but live it up today. Anna decided then, "It's done, better to let it lay." She turned to give her a hug. "I hope you'll both be very happy. We'll miss you." "You won't miss me Mama, I'm not going far, and Joe is teaching me how to drive the automobile, so I'll be coming to town a lot. I'll drive you anyplace you want to go."

Margaret ran up the stairs to grab some clothes, "Keep my room like it is, and keep Dorothy out of it. I'll get my things from time to time as I need them." The screen door banged shut behind them, the mantel clock donged one o'clock in the morning, and Anna and Dow started up the stairs. How quickly your life could change in an hour's time. "I'm going to miss her so." Anna whispered. "No, you won't, she was always traveling here and there, in and out of the house anyway. You may see more of her than before. She'll need you for recipes, sewing and such," replied Dow. "Yes, that's true," and suddenly she saw things differently. "She will need help and advice on household matters, and my kitchen recipes. I need to make her some aprons. Where did I put those pieces of leftover material?"

Anna could tell that Dow was agitated and wanted to talk something over with her. Her first thought, he wants to move again. Sure enough, after they had gone to bed he told her he had a chance to rent a farm down on the Liberty Pike. He wanted to farm again, and Mollie was selling the plumbing shop. He had been staying on just to keep it going for her. They had only been here on Eighteenth Street for a year and she had liked it. She liked the convenience of town living.

Anna hated this move to begin with, and as time went by, it only got worse. There was a creek that ran in front of the place, and a swinging bridge to get over it. Other farms in the area were better situated, such as the Pardieck's farm that sat high on a hill, and the farm of the Nocton family. Dorothy was seldom at home, choosing to spend her time with the two little Nocton girls. The creek would be a dry bed sometimes, and at others, raging torrents, out of its banks flooding everything. "Find another place Dow. I don't like it here," Anna told him. At the end of the season, he did.

Anna packed her household, personal belongings, and they moved to Webster, Indiana. It was a very small settlement consisting of a general store and school. The house was constructed with painted brick. The big white barn sat across from it on the opposite side of the road. Jack and Jenny, the pair of white mules, was Dow's pride and joy that pulled one wagon, while Kate and Belle, the huge black Percheron workhorses, pulled another.

Anna got her family settled once more and enrolled the children in school, starting Joann for the first time. Joann didn't want to go. She would start each morning with her complaints, "I don't feel good today, Papa" Dow would then tell Anna, "better keep her at home today." Dow would go out to the barn and Joann would make a quick recovery and start to play. Anna could see how this was going and decided to put an end to it.

"I don't feel good today, Papa," Joann started the next morning, at breakfast. Before Dow could say a word, Anna leaned over and felt her forehead with the palm of her hand. "I do believe she has a touch of fever and needs to be put right back in bed with a big dose of Castor Oil, She's been sick most of this week." She took Joann from the table and led her back to her room and settled her in bed. In a few minutes, she was back with a large spoon and a bottle of Castor Oil. Joann eyed the bottle and spoon and shook her head,

"I feel much better now." Anna smiled, just as she thought, but she administered the dose and said, "There, that should have you up and around feeling fine by tomorrow. A quiet day in bed should do it." She walked over to the window and pulled down the shade leaving the room dark and gloomy on such a lovely day.

The next morning Anna found Joann at the breakfast table dressed and ready for her day at school. Dow looked her over and asked, "How are you feeling today?" Joann answered, "I feel fine Papa, just fine." Dow came to the breakfast table and said to Anna, "I've made up my mind; I'm going to sell the mules to Mr. Teamen up the road. He's offered me a good price for them and we could use the money right now. I don't really need them since I've got the team of horses." "Whatever you want to do Dow, that is your decision to make," Anna told him, as she poured his coffee from the blue granite pot. "However, I didn't think anything would make you part with those mules, you've always been so crazy about them."

Midmorning, Anna watched from the window as Mr. Teamen left with the mules. She also saw the expression on Dow's face when he entered the kitchen awhile later. She knew that sometimes, even when it made good sense; it didn't make it easy to do. She knew how he felt about those mules.

The next morning, Anna could see that Dow was not in a hurry to go to the barn. He didn't want to see those empty stalls. He did go with his head down and slid one of the huge doors to the side and entered the barn. He looked where he expected to see empty stalls, he couldn't believe his eyes. There stood the mules as usual waiting for their feed. He ran forward to pat their silky necks, "well; well, now just how did you manage this?" He looked to see where they had gotten in, and saw that the side door had been left open by one of the boys. The mules had come home. He didn't know how they had accomplished it, but they had. It wasn't long before Mr. Teaman come looking for them. "It seems we're going to have a problem with these mules." Dow nodded his head in agreement and asked, "how about, I just buy them back? It seems this is where they've made up their minds to be." "I agree," said Mr. Teamen and accepted his money back. When Dow told Anna about the mules he said, "Those mules are real smart. They knew they had a good home here and decided to come back to it. I will never part with Jack and Jenny again."

The new year of 1925 rang in a bitterly cold winter. Anna made use of these shut-in months to catch up on her needle work. Her hands were busy with everyday mending or darning socks. She cut quilt squares from old scraps of material left over from dresses or aprons and then sewed them together until she had enough to make the quilt. Flour and feed sacks were bleached out in the sun, by her, laying the pieces, on the grass, in the hot sunshine. She now made trimming, for to use as tea towels for kitchen use. Anna was thrifty and nothing went to waste.

In February, eight-year-old Lorenzo came home from school, sick with fever and a croupy cough. She put everything else aside and tended him night and day. The doctor said the dreaded word "Diphtheria." She had been through this nightmare before. Through the weeks of tending the illness, there came a day of hope. The family was together for a Sunday afternoon, and Lorenzo wanted to get out of bed and join them. They wrapped him, warmly in a blanket, and Anna held him on her lap.

He enjoyed this, and suddenly he sat straight and alert and said to them, "Open the door!" Fred told him, "no, we can't, it's cold and snowing outside." Lorenzo insisted, "But you must let them in." "Who?" they asked. Lorenzo was becoming so excited that Anna said to humor him and open the door for just a minute. She wrapped the blanket more snuggly about him. His eyes seemed to be following something around the room that no one else was seeing. Anna asked him, "What is it?" Her heart gripped in fear when he answered, "Don't you see them? There are Mama Angels, and Papa Angels and even baby Angels." His eyes looked back to the door, and he said, "They're leaving now, the pretty Angel wants me to come with her, she's holding out her arms for me." His little blond head fell back against Anna's breast and she knew he was dead. He had gone with the pretty angel. "Oh Lord, how can I go through this again? My heart broke when I lost Roland, and now you've taken our darling Lorenzo. He was always so good; he was an angel with us always."

It was another funeral and another little boy gone, to join his brother in Lutherania, next to their grandparents. Anna stood in the cold, by the graveside and cried, "Look after him Mama."

Lorenzo

CHAPTER 19

TWISTS AND TURNS

Margaret came to visit often, and helped Anna through her grieving period. They consoled one another. She began to bring a young neighbor of hers with her to visit. They had tea in the afternoon and sewed together, exchanging patterns and quilt pieces. Anna liked Irene Sieweick, and so did Wayne. He began asking her out on dates, much to her father's dismay. Her father objected to her going with anyone. As usually happens, they would find a way to see each other and be together anyway. Margaret was the go-between and helped them to see each other, most of the time at her home.

Wayne and Irene decided to elope, and Margaret and Joe helped them. They drove them to a Justice of the Peace, out of town, and stood up with them as witnesses. On the way home, Irene suddenly thought of what she had done, and what her father was going to say about it and began to cry. Wayne looked to Margaret to figure things out as she always did. "We'll go to Mom and Pop, and Mom will take care of everything," Margaret assured him.

It was after supper, when the four of them came trouping in to tell what they had done. Anna made coffee and sandwiches and they sat at the kitchen table deciding what to do next. Anna told them, "what's done is done; it's too late now to cry over spilt milk. Margaret, you should not have gotten yourself into this, but since you have, I suggest you be the messenger of the tidings to the Sieweick's. Irene can write a note to her folks about the marriage, and that they will be staying with us for awhile. They will know where she is and when they get over the shock, and come to terms with it, they can come or send a message to her." This as it came to pass, was exactly what Anna hoped. All was forgiven, and Wayne was accepted into the family as a favored son in-law.

It was the end of May. The day had started clear with a sunny day. Anna had been working in the garden for quite awhile. Her special roses had buds, the irises were in full bloom of purple and yellow, and the peonies were a variety of pink, red and white with their large fragrant blooms. She noticed it had become cloudy and overcast and the breeze had a sudden chill to it. She got up from her kneeling position, where she had been weeding, and looked over the fields. The sky in the distance had a greenish cast. She saw Dow coming from the barn with Dorothy right behind him. He came to stand beside Anna and he also surveyed the fields in the distance. A spattering of rain drops started and the wind increased. "Let's get to the house," Dow shouted.

When they were in the shelter, of the back porch, they stopped and looked out at the coming storm. The rest of the family joined them there. A rumbling noise in the distance startled Dow and reminded him of another storm, in another place, when he was a young boy in Iowa. Then he saw it coming across the far distant field, the black twisting funnel kicking up clouds of dust. "Get to the cellar," Dow yelled at them. "There goes Finley's barn."

Dorothy stayed at the window, awe struck at the sight she was seeing. "I want to see," she cried. Dow pulled her with him as they fled down to the cellar that led from the door off the kitchen.

They waited, thinking, the house might be coming down on them at any time. Dow told them of the many times, in Iowa, they had gone down into the storm cellar, his mother had his father dig for them, and was why she had insisted they leave Iowa and come to farm in Indiana. She had crossed the prairie in a covered wagon, putting up with hardships on the trail. She had put up with Indians, invading her home whenever they chose, but she was scared of the tornadoes and how suddenly they could appear with no warning. It was the only thing he knew that ever got the best of his mother.

Dow started up the cellar steps to check on the outcome of the storm. He came back to give the "all clear." "Nothing of ours has been touched. I'm going to check on our neighbors," he called down to them.

Anna went back to her garden to see the irises lying flat, along with the peonies and other plants, but her roses had stood the storm just fine. They were minus some of their petals, on the full blooms, but the buds were still intact. She sent up a prayer in thanks to the lord that they were kept safe.

Dorothy was sick, terribly sick, and Anna sent for the doctor. "It's Typhoid Fever, I'm sure of it," he related to her. "How did she get it? Our water has always been good here," asked Anna. "Let's talk to her about where she's been and what she's gotten into," said Dr. Bond.

"Dorothy, where have you been lately and what did you eat or drink?" asked Dr. Bond on entering the sick room. Dorothy held her throbbing head in her hands. "I went to the doings they had out at the Fair Grounds. I drank some water out of the horse tank." "Oh no!" Anna let out, as she sank into the chair by the bed. "She's going to have a rough time of it, and so will you," the doctor told Anna. He spent a lot of time explaining the illness and its stages, and how to nurse her along with it. He left medicine with instructions for dosage.

For several weeks Anna hardly slept. She was afraid she was going to lose another child. Dorothy talked out of her head; she didn't know Margaret, when she came to see her. At last, the fever broke and day by day she improved. Her hair fell out and she was bald, her skin shed in flakes. Anna put newspapers on the floor for her to stand on when she wiped her down with cool damp cloths. The papers that held the flaking, of the skin, were carefully disposed of by burning.

Over time, Dorothy's body renewed itself with new skin and hair that came back blonde and curly. Anna and Dow had been through another rough spell in their life and seen it through together.

March of 1926, Anna turned Fifty years old. They had just moved into, what she considered a dream place. It was located on the Union Pike and it had the name, "Pinehurst Farm." The house set back from the road, with tall pine trees in the front yard. The house was painted white with dark green shutters, at the windows. The interior was spacious and decorated with fluted woodwork and rosettes, working fireplaces, and built-in cupboards for her dishes in the dining room.

After five moves, in five years, and all she had been through, she decided Dow would have a hard time of it, to move her from here. She set in, making this house her own. She unboxed her belongings, that she hadn't taken the trouble to, with the other places. She displayed the vases and pretty dishes; she loved so much, and got out her best linen. In a side yard, in view from the wrap around porch, she selected the spot for her garden. Her roses had been uprooted and reset so many times, but had survived. Each one had a special memory, such as the two, from Joe Hill himself.

The only thing that could get Anna, the least bit upset, these days, were the visits of Dow's niece Jesse and her husband Ivan. She had always found Jesse overbearing, and her husband wasn't any better. She had said to Dow, "He's so tight he squeaks, they're quite a pair; Ivan holds the penny while Jesse pinches it!" Margaret would leave when they appeared; she hadn't forgotten the incident about her "Pancake" hat and being called "Piggy." All of a sudden, it seemed they began to make frequent visits to "Uncle Dow," and especially on Sunday afternoons.

When Anna arrived home from her visit to the cemetery, she would find them sitting on the front porch. She never knew how they got there, for, they didn't own a car. They would stay until after supper and one of the boys would have to drive them back to Richmond.

On occasion, Jesse would bring "Uncle Dow" a small package of cheese, "because he is so fond of it," Jesse would coo. Taking the package to the kitchen, and unwrapping it, Anna would be disgusted to find a single slice, tissue paper thin. Fred had overheard Jesse on one occasion, when he had driven them home. Jesse asked him to come in and get a piece of meatloaf to take home with him. Ivan had gone to the kitchen and Jesse had called out to him, "Slice it thin, Ivan!" When Fred got home with it and told the family, they all laughed, and it became the saying, in the family, when anyone was carving meat.

"This Sunday, I'm going to have things differently," thought Anna. "I'm going to be gone this afternoon Dow, after we leave the cemetery the children and I are going to Ellie Engleberts. I plan to have just a light supper tonight, but I'll be home in plenty of time to lay it out."

Anna enjoyed her visit with Ellie, promising to get together again soon and started for home. As soon as she entered the house, she detected the odor of fried chicken. She went in a bee-line, straight to her kitchen, not even stopping to remove her hat. "What's going on here?" Jesse was just removing an apron and answered, "Why, we were just sitting down to supper. I had Uncle Dow kill a couple of chickens and I fried them up. Oh, but I saved you some in the warming oven," Jesse motioned toward the big range. Anna walked over to the warming oven and jerked open the door. There on the platter were the necks and the backs of the chickens. Anna was furious. She removed the platter from the oven and slammed the door. She then walked to the table and took that platter of chicken, as well as the bowls of vegetables and gravy and removed them from the table. Jesse stood there aghast, "what are you doing? We were about to eat." Anna began to reset the table, and answered her with, "when we eat here, we all eat together!"

It was an uncomfortable meal for some of them. When Dow saw the fire in Anna's eyes, he knew he was in trouble for killing the chickens and allowing Jesse in her kitchen. Ivan however enjoyed the meal with gusto, leaving a plateful of chicken bones picked clean.

Dorothy knew her mama was tired of Jesse and Ivan and this Sunday she was going to get the best of them. Her chance came, when Ivan got up from his rest out on the porch and announced he was hungry for watermelon. Fred said he knew of a place close by, selling some nice melons. Ivan said, "Let's go get some to eat this afternoon." Fred got out his car and Dorothy went along with them to select the watermelons. Dow picked out several melons, and Ivan picked out two for him and placed them in the backseat of the car and covered them with the lap robe. He planned to take his melons home with him when Fred drove them home that night.

Everyone gathered on the porch and the watermelon party began. The melons were delicious, red, ripe and juicy. With several people eating, it wasn't long before all the melons that Dow had bought had been sliced and eaten, with Jesse and Ivan enjoying a large share, and looking for more. "Is that all the melons?" Ivan asked. Dorothy knew about his melons in the back of the car. She told him, "No, there's more out back. I'll go get them." She brought in the melons from the back of the car and they were sliced and eaten, Jesse made a comment, "I think these are the best ones yet." Dorothy laughed and agreed with her as she helped herself to another slice.

Fred was a bit suspicious at Dorothy's actions and discovered what she had done. When he had the chance to speak to her alone he said, "You're going to be in trouble when they find those melons gone." "Well, I don't care," she said, "They ate up all of ours and asked for more, so I got them more. They come out here every Sunday for Mama to feed them a big Sunday dinner and Jesse never helps with the dishes either. Maybe if they get mad they will stay away!" Dorothy didn't get in trouble and the visits from Jesse and Ivan continued, in good weather at least.

Train Depot

CHAPTER 20

FLO'S VISIT

Dow was at the train depot, to pick up his sister Flo. Fred had driven Wayne's car and they had allowed plenty of time. "You might know, when we're on time, the train would be late," Dow stated. They left the waiting area and walked out to the platform, Fred replied, "I think it's coming now." The huge black steam engine had slowed with a screeching of brakes and exhausting steam, and was passing the station so that the passenger cars would be positioned for the passengers to alight all along the platform.

The conductor opened the door, of one of the cars, and put down the steps. Baggage carts were started out, down the platform to the rear of the train, to the baggage car. Dow was looking left and right, not knowing which car she would be coming from. "I hope she knows us," Dow remarked. "Oh, she'll know you, but she won't know me," Fred answered. He was nineteen and considered himself a man now. "I don't think I'll know her, it's been a long time since I've seen her."

Flo emerged from a car, a little way down the platform. As

she stepped down from the train, she got many appraising looks from men and women alike, for she was a striking figure for a small town. She wore a black traveling suit that showed a very trim petite figure. Her black hair was perfectly coifed into an up-do, swept up and pinned, a perky hat with veil sat atop. She clutched her black bag, and looked around for the brother she was expecting to see. He saw her first, "there she is and she hasn't changed a bit."

She came to them smiling, and extended her hand to Dow and Fred. They were not a family to display affection in public, or in private either, for that matter. Fred got her matching set of luggage and sat it on the backseat next to her. Fred started the car and headed it across the Doran Bridge and to the north of Richmond to Union Pike. "We're on a nice farm, it's called Pinehurst, Anna loves it there," Dow informed her. "Some of the family has left home for homes of their own. Margaret's married to a real nice man. You'll see them tomorrow night, they're coming to dinner. Wayne's married too, rascal eloped on us and he's farming his father-in-law's place. This is his car, he loaned it to me, to come get you." "That's right," Flo remarked, "you never did learn to drive or own a car did you?" "No," Dow laughed, "I just drive my mules; there are none better than my Jack and Jenny."

Fred turned the car into the long lane with tall pine trees lining both sides. The big white house gleamed in the distance. The lane extended even further beyond where they were stopping to the barn and other out-buildings. When he pulled up to a walkway, that led to the front porch, and helped his aunt from the car, she remarked, "my, this is a nice place, no wonder Anna loves it here." "She's done a lot with the place herself, she loves to garden you know." That was more of a statement than a question by Dow.

Anna heard the car drive up and met them in the front hallway. Fred passed her with the luggage on his way up the staircase to the quest room she had ready. "It's so nice to see you Flo, you look lovely and you haven't changed a bit in all these years." "Blame it on the Mississippi humidity; it's good for the complexion," Flo remarked. Anna led the way into the parlor for Flo to greet the family at home.

Leonard stood up and offered her his comfortable chair. "Well, Leonard, you've grown up to be a fine looking young man, all that curly hair. I hear your younger brother beat you to the altar. What's the matter, don't you like girls?" "Just not the right one come along yet," he replied, and found a seat a good distance away.

Virling was sitting back in a far corner of the room when Anna mentioned his name to Flo and told her he was seventeen now. "I remember, he was your "preemie" wasn't he?" Flo gave him no more than a glance and then her eyes fastened on fourteen year old Dorothy. "Look at all that long blonde hair; I must give you a good hair cut while I'm here." Dorothy didn't say a word, but she thought, "Like hell you will!"

Last to be introduced, for the first time, was Joann, who headed for her Papa's lap as soon as he sat down. Flo said to her, "so, you're the little girl named after my mother Kiziah?" Joann shook her head no, "my name is Joann." "No," Aunt Flo remarked to her, "Joann is your middle name, Kiziah is your first name and I will call you Kiziah."

Everyone went back to whatever they had been doing when their guest had arrived. Dow excused himself and the boys and went back to their farm chores. Anna went back to her preparations for a special dinner. Flo said she needed some rest, from her long journey, and chose a comfortable wicker rocking chair on the porch. She picked up the book she had brought along to read, but she was too distracted by her surroundings. From inside the house came the clink of china being put on the long table in the dining room, next the tinkling crash of the silverware being added.

From the barn, came the whiney of the horses, feeding time for them too. The little white terrier, Bonnie, was barking at something down by the woods, a rabbit perhaps, she had come across on her way back to the house.

The porch was cool and pleasant, on such a hot summer day, as it had been. The delicious aroma of fried chicken wafted through the screen door. Flo set aside the book she had just been leafing through and settled back in the rocking chair to look out on the spacious green lawn and the lofty darker green of the pine trees. "It is so peaceful here; no wonder Anna loves it so. I hope Dow will settle here, he has uprooted her enough, Flo thought.

Saturday morning was always a busy morning for Anna, that one especially so. She had made preparations for the big dinner party she was having that night for Flo. Margaret and Joe were coming, as well as, Irene and Wayne.

Flo came down to breakfast to find a table laden with stacks of golden pancakes, fluffy scrambled eggs, and a platter heaped with crisp bacon. Flo sipped a cup of black coffee and refused anything more.

After breakfast, she insisted on helping wash the dishes, however; Dorothy stood by with a towel to dry. All of a sudden she exclaimed, "Oh, Aunt Flo, your lovely silk scarf is dangling in the dish pan!" Flo removed her scarf from around her neck and flung it to a near by kitchen chair. "No matter," she replied, "there's more where that come from." Dorothy thought to herself, "She must be rich, like they say she is, to do that with expensive things." Shortly after, Flo remembered she wanted to cut Dorothy's hair and set out to get scissors and comb. Dorothy headed to the barn loft, where she stayed until it was time to come in and get ready for the special supper.

Margaret and Joe arrived first and sat in the parlor for a while to get reacquainted with her aunt. She introduced her husband and Flo thought he was charming. Flo later remarked to Anna that she wondered how Margaret had gotten such a handsome, good looking, husband when she was somewhat a bit too plump herself, or was she expecting?

When Anna and Dow talked that night after they were settled in bed, Anna said, "Well, Flo has managed to insult each one of us, except you so far, and your daughter will probably stay in the barn until she leaves.

The next morning, after the usual Sunday breakfast, Anna went to her rose garden. She selected an array of colors to arrange into nice bouquets to take for her weekly visit to Lutherania Cemetery. Flo was dressed for an outing, so she accompanied Anna. Fred brought the car around and helped them into it. Fred placed the flowers next to him on the front seat. "It's a lovely day for a drive; I understand you go every Sunday Anna." Anna nodded, "Yes, all but the days when the weather doesn't permit." Fred drove the car the familiar route to the cemetery, through the gates and to the right of the chapel. He stopped at the sight of the narrow obelisk tombstone that had been erected for his Grandparents. Anna gathered her bouquets and going first to her little sons graves, knelt and placed the roses in the vases she left there for that purpose. Fred hurried off, to fill a can of water. It hurt him to see the pain of loss she underwent each time.

"I wish you could have seen them Flo, my darling boys, Roland was only Four years old, and he slipped away from me so quick and Lorenzo only eight when the angels came for him. I ask myself, "Why must this be?" Each week, I bring them roses to let them know they are not forgotten." She rose and went to her parent's grave and then to her brothers, leaving the roses each time in her ritual.

Flo placed her hand on Anna's arm, "I'm sorry you've been through such a rough time of it. Maybe it would have turned out better for you if he had married Hazel instead." Flo suddenly realized she had misspoke. Anna jerked her head up, "That's alright Flo, I know about her, and she won't be bothering us anymore." She started toward the car leaving Flo to always wonder what had occurred. Fred started the car and headed for home. He always wanted to oblige her on these weekly visits, but he was glad when he could get back home.

Flo started out her week by being up early on Monday, having her usual cup of black coffee, while the rest of the family had the substantial farm breakfast, Anna made for them each day. Today was laundry day and Virling was preparing the wash tubs, filling them with water for rinsing the clothes and the washing machine with hot water. It was a fine day for hanging wash, on the line, in the backyard. Anna enjoyed her work. The sheets came off the line bleached white by the sun and smelling fresh from drying in the warm breeze.

In the latter part of the afternoon, Flo decided she would pop some popcorn for later in the evening. She found some large pans in the pantry and filled them with the butter and salted popcorn and sat them on the sideboard in the dining room. She found a book to read from the bookcase and settled herself comfortably in the parlor. She heard laughter coming from the boys as they entered the house from being in the fields all afternoon. As Leonard and Fred passed through the dining room, they saw the appetizing popcorn, and being hungry they helped themselves to handfuls of the delicious grains. Flo rushed into the room, shouting at them, "Stop that!" Get your dirty hands out of that popcorn. I popped that for later this evening." Dow had followed the boys into the room, with Anna right behind him. Flo turned to them, "Look what they're doing, eating out of the pan and they've been with those mules all afternoon."

Anna had all she could take of Flo by this time, so she spoke her piece. "My boys can have all the popcorn they want. I planted that popcorn, I grew it myself. I shelled it, and I saw them wash their hands, as they always do when coming in from the fields." Dow then cut in to speak his mind, "The boys worked hard all afternoon and they were hungry when they came in, and as to those mules that seem to bother you, well, they may be mules, but you Flo, are an Ass! Pack your bags tonight, because I'm taking you to the station in the morning."

CHAPTER 21

SCHOOL DAZE

Anna was happy; everything was going well for a change. This farm had been doing the best for them. So well in fact, that Dow had bought a threshing machine of his own. Anna looked out the upstairs window that faced the barn and other out buildings. She had heard the sound of voices and the rattle of chains. She pulled back the curtains for a better view in time to see Dow arguing with a man, and then heading for the house. She hurried down the back stairs and entered the kitchen as Dow came through the door, banging the screen door behind him. "What's the matter? Who's that man?" Anna rushed the questions at him. "He's from the implement company, brought a dray to load up the threshing machine, says I didn't pay for it," Dow answered. "But you did, you have the receipt for it in your strong box," stated Anna. "I know, and I'm going to get it and show it to him before he leaves with the machine. He's loading it up, and it's a lot of work," Dow remarked.

Dow opened his strong box and took out his receipt showing the implement paid in full. He put it in his shirt pocket and returned to the barnyard. The men had just finished loading the heavy equipment on the dray and chaining it down. Dow walked up to the man in charge, who hadn't believed him, handed over the receipt and watched the look on his face pale, then turn beet red, when he ordered the men to unload it. Dow felt sorry for the men doing the work, but he also knew they were being paid for a job that wasn't necessary. That was a loss to the company, but maybe they would be more careful before they accused someone of not paying in the future. Dow returned to the house and put his receipt away in his strong box. He told Anna, "It's a good thing I had my proof right here or I would have been out of a threshing machine"

Dorothy got on the school hack at the end of the long lane of Pinehurst Farm. She had books and lunch pail in her arms. She found a seat next to her best friend, Audrey Ashcraft and the hack proceeded down the road. Everything was always peaceful until the hack stopped to pick up a bully. Once Buster Thorp got on the hack, he started trouble of some sort. He would snatch the little boy's hat, pull the girls hair, mess up their books or their lunch. He usually left Dorothy alone, but this morning, he felt like giving her a kick on the leg as he passed by her seat. "Oww, that hurt, you better watch it Buster," Dorothy complained.

All day, Dorothy was reminded of the kick because her leg hurt, and it now showed a bruise. When they boarded the hack after school, again finding a seat together with Audrey, the girls began to talk. Buster got on, pushing a young girl ahead of him by the nape of the neck, hurting her and making her cry. Dorothy felt she must intervene; she had enough of his bullying. "Leave her alone," she shouted at him! He turned to Dorothy and sneered, "Kiss my ass!" Dorothy reached to the seat behind her and picked up her empty milk bottle. "Okay, You asked for it, you got it!"

she said and brought the milk bottle crashing down on his head. The bottle didn't break, but it brought about a dazed and subdued look to his face. He was still holding his head as he got off at his stop. Audrey said to Dorothy in a worried voice, "I'm afraid you're going to be in trouble over that."

The next day, a meeting was held in the principal's office to "get to the bottom" of what had taken place on the school hack. Dorothy didn't mince words, "he told me to "Kiss his ass!" and I kissed it for him, my way," she told the principal. When the matter was cleared up, Dorothy was not punished in any way, and Buster was transferred to another school. Military School was advised. Dow and Anna looked at each other and shook their heads, "My, that girl does have a temper!"

It was late afternoon; the sky had become overcast with a hint of rain in the air. Anna went out onto the porch to see if there was any sign of the school hack approaching. It was past the time for it and she was beginning to worry. She walked out on the lawn and followed a path to the barnyard gate. She saw Leonard preparing to round up the cows for the evening milking. She called to him and he came running. "Could you take the car and check the roads the school hack takes? It should have been here by now." Leonard left his mother by the gate and ran to the garage for the car. He didn't drive very often; he usually left the motors to Fred. He preferred the horses himself. He turned to the right onto Union Pike and followed it out to the intersection of a main highway, and as he approached a curve he saw the school hack overturned in the ditch. Children of all ages, standing, sitting by the road, some crying, some were still in the hack trying to get out. The hack driver seemed to be in a daze, holding his head and leaning against a wheel.

Leonard began searching for Dorothy and Joann. He then got

a glimpse of Dorothy's reddish blonde hair, coming up and out of the side of the hack. She climbed out, and reached back in to lift her little sister to safety. He saw Joann had a gash in her forehead, and was bleeding from it. She had also lost a shoe. He ran to them. Dorothy shouted for him when she saw him coming. "I had a time of it, I couldn't find her. She had a seat on top of her." Leonard reached for Joann and she held on to her big brothers neck tightly. Dorothy scrambled and slid from the side of the hack. "What a mess, I don't think anyone is hurt bad, someone came by and went for help. I'm sure glad you showed up when you did."

Leonard led her to the car, "Mom sent me to look for you, and she was worried when the hack didn't come as usual." He placed Joann on the back seat. "Don't you have a clean handkerchief we can put on her head? All I've got is a red bandana, and I wouldn't want to use that, I've been in the fields all day." Dorothy produced hers, still clean and unused since her mother had tucked it in her pocket that very morning, her question every morning as they left for school and church, "do you have a clean handkerchief?" Leonard started the car as a few drops of rain spattered the windshield. Help was now arriving for the others. Let's get her home and Mom can do something with that gash."

Anna had been watching the road anxiously from the porch. She was relieved to see the car come up the lane with its passengers. Leonard carried Joann to the porch, "I'll put the car away and then I'll be in. It's starting to rain," shouted Leonard on his run back to the car.

Anna removed the handkerchief and examined the bloody gash in Joann's forehead. She cleaned and dressed it as best she could with Joann wincing and crying out that, "It hurt." "I must tend to this, and hope you aren't left with a scar." She turned to inspect Dorothy standing by. "Are you sure you're not hurt anywhere?" "Not a scratch," replied Dorothy happily. Leonard returned to his mother, to see if he was needed further, and seeing everyone calm and taken care of, he went back to his evening chores.

It was a thankful family that sat around the dinner table that evening. "Wonder what caused the hack to go in the ditch? Was anyone else on the road?" asked Fred. "Perhaps something broke on the steering apparatus." he added. "The driver looked pretty shook up to me" commented Leonard. "I wouldn't be surprised if he quit the route after this." Dow spoke up, "Well now, if he does quit, that might just be the opportunity Wayne's looking for. He needs a part time job to bring in a few extra dollars besides the farm."

Anna lay beside Dow listening to the patter of rain on the roof. She was happy to have her children safe. What a day it had been. Wayne got the job to drive the school hack. Dorothy was happy about this. She sat right behind him and told him all the news, of the family, each day. It was known to all the other students, this was her seat, and her brother was the driver.

It was warm inside the hack, when she got on after school, so she opened her window beside her. Wayne already had his window open and a pretty young teacher was talking and smiling to him. This irritated Dorothy, so she began to act up, as she usually did when things didn't suit her. She tossed her head back and laughed and grabbed Wayne's hat off his head. The teacher glared at her and spoke to her in an angry voice, "You get off this instant! I'm taking you to the principal's office!" Dorothy glared back at the teacher and replied in a sassy voice, "This is my brother and I can do as I want. You better leave him alone, He's married and I'll tell his wife you've been making eyes at him." Fortunately for Wayne, everyone was on the hack and he was ready to pull out. His face was red as a beet as he drove away. The teacher was left standing with a look of, "what just happened here?" She had been bested by a teenager. Dorothy sat, with a smug look on her face, "I guess I fixed her, she won't be out there making "goo-goo" eyes at him anymore!"

Glenn Miller Park

CHAPTER 22

LEONARD TAKES A WIFE

The day dawned on a perfect Fourth of July. Anna was already in the kitchen frying the many chickens that would be devoured that day, along with the potato salad, sliced tomatoes, just picked from the garden, fresh baked bread with churned butter, and several layer cakes and pies.

Anna left the hampers; she was packing with food, to look out the screened door to the backyard, and further back, to the barnyard, to see if Dow was bringing the team of horses, hitched to the wagon. One horse would do, but Kate and Belle liked to be together as a team. Since they were not in view, as yet, probably getting a brush applied to their backs, to look their well groomed best, on the road today. Dow would be putting red tassels on their harness to dress them up.

Anna stepped out into the warm sunlight, to breathe in the fresh fragrant air, and inspect the blooms of the morning glories blooming, on the trellis, by the back door. It was a beautiful day and Anna was happy. She was excited with the plans for the day. A picnic in the park was special. She had to get back to the kitchen and turn the fryers over, so with one more deep breath of the lovely outdoors she reluctantly went back inside.

This would be almost a family reunion, for her sisters and their families would be there, and some of Dow's family too. She knew she could count on Jesse and Ivan being there if food was involved. Margaret and Joe would be joining them, as well as Wayne and Irene and a couple of the Siweicke girls. Irene's sisters were fun and she enjoyed having them.

Leonard had gone downstairs, in a new bow tie, and light tan cap. He was twenty seven years old and still single. He was going to bring a girl to the picnic for them to meet today. Actually, she was going to Glen Miller Park with her parents and would meet him there. Anna gave him an approving glance, as she packed the last of the picnic fare. "I almost forgot the pickles, my, but you look nice, it seems to take a girl for you boys to spruce up." "Now, Mama, it's a special day, Fourth of July and all." Leonard grinned and picked up one of the hampers. "This is heavy; you must have packed enough for an army." "Enough for our crowd, and extra that might happen by," she told him.

At last, everyone was in the wagon, and set off for the park. As Dow entered the park at the main entrance, on National Road, Virling and Joann wanted to stop and get a drink from the spring. They insisted this water always tasted better than any other, and they liked going down the stone steps and drinking from the pipe. When he got them loaded up again, they began to decide what part of the park to picnic in. "I think we'll take that shady spot overlooking the lake, everyone knows it's my favorite since I was a little girl," Anna told him. Dow grinned at her, "I remember taking you out on that lake in a canoe, and you had on a white dress with a matching parasol." Anna laughed, "You still remember that, after all these years, I was just a girl on Tenth Street."

They were soon joined at their "spot" by other members of the family. Along came Jesse and Ivan with a small basket, "We'll just have ours over here," said Jesse and indicated they would not be sharing their basket with the group.

When the time came to spread the picnic fare, everyone opened their baskets and set out the food to share. Thelma, Irene's sister, had a way with pastry, and she set out a large layer cake, thick with fudge frosting. Irene had made "Shoo-fly" pie, with flaky crusts, and brown sugary fillings. Margaret and Joe had the ice cream freezer full of homemade Vanilla ice cream. Anna unpacked the hampers filled with the fried chicken and all the other foods, and everyone heaped their plates and enjoyed this feast.

Jesse had opened her basket and set them out a dainty sandwich and a boiled egg. Ivan kept looking over at the fried chicken and potato salad heaped on everybody's plate. Anna glanced his way, he reminded her of a hungry dog, licking his chops. She took pity on him and she said, "Ivan, won't you have some of this chicken? I made so much and I wouldn't want it to go to waste." He got up and hurried over with his plate. "Well now, I don't mind if I do, it sure looks delicious Aunt Anna." He now dropped down to a spot closer in, to eat with them. Jesse stayed where she was.

Leonard left the group, to find "his girl." Dorothy was curious as to what she would look like, and waited impatiently for his return. Finally, her wait was over, when he appeared with a very young and frail looking girl hanging on his arm. "Everyone," he shouted, "this is Mary Tharp." She began to giggle as he led her first to his Mom and Pop, then to his Sisters and Brothers, Aunts, Uncles and cousins. He soon left with her, still hanging onto his arm and giggling. Dorothy was the first to speak up, "well, what does he see in her? She's such a silly little thing." Anna reached out and put her hand on Dorothy's arm, to quiet her, "she's your brother's friend, so say no more about it." Dorothy could tell the others were just as shocked as she was. Leonard was twenty-seven years old, this girl was only seventeen.

That night, as Anna tried to find a comfortable position in her bed, and had done a good bit of tossing and turning, Dow knew she had Leonard on her mind. She finally said to him, "do you think he can be serious about that little girl? Think of the difference in their ages." Dow answered her with, "think of the difference in "our" ages, that's what worried your parents, remember?" "Well, she seems younger, and acts so silly as Dorothy said," Anna answered.

Dow then, filled her in on what he knew, "I know Ida and Ollie Tharp. Ida was a Kendrick, and an only child, and so is Mary. She has had a sheltered life, they always kept to themselves. Things work out as they will, so try to put it out of your mind for now, and try to get some sleep."

The Holiday Season was approaching. Anna was busier than ever. First came Thanksgiving, with a feast that she loved to prepare for her family. She was making her shopping list, for the spices she would need, as well as the staple items that were always kept on hand. She heard the front door open and shut with a bang. Leonard came into the parlor with Mary, again hanging on his arm possessively. By the looks on their faces, "something was in the wind," she thought.

"Where's Pop," asked Leonard, as he crossed the room to the fireplace to warm his hands by the flickering flames. "He's out in the kitchen getting some coffee," Anna answered. "He should be back in a minute." She started to rise from her chair, "I'll bring you in some to warm you up." Leonard stopped her, "no, not just yet, I want to talk to you first."

Mary had removed her scarf and unbuttoned her drab

looking, grayish green coat. "Take off your coat Mary, and come sit down," Anna said to her with a warm smile. Mary very timidly moved to the sofa, and sat perched on the edge of the seat. She beckoned for Leonard to join her and he sank into its depth's and was comfortable, or as comfortable as he could be under the circumstances.

Dow entered the room, "well, I see we have company. How are you, Mary?" "Fine," Mary said with a weak little grin. Leonard then sat up and perched on the edge of the seat with Mary. "I don't know how to tell you this, except to come right out with it and tell you, I got married to Mary this afternoon down at Judge Potter's office across from the court house." He didn't know why he mentioned the location; they knew Judge Potter as the Justice of the Peace there for a long time.

Anna and Dow looked at each other, and then at the couple on the sofa. Dow said, "Well, now that the cat is out of the bag, what are your plans?" Leonard looked to Dow for answers, "we don't know what to do now, Mary is afraid to go home and tell her folks." Anna spoke up, "she must, and they have got to know. You have made your decision to marry, so now, you must get on with your announcements of it. I hope they will take the news well. After you have delivered your news, you're welcome to come back here for supper, and Leonard, I will see that your room is ready for your bride. You will need a few days to make your plans for a home of your own."

"Thanks Mom, that helps a lot. We'll go on right now and get it over with." He pulled Mary to her feet and bundled her into her ugly coat and scarf, and shrugged into his own heavy jacket, as he went through the hall to the front door. When the door closed with a bang, Anna felt that bang in her heart. Her first born son, with his cute smile, and curly brown hair, it never took much to make him happy. He was twenty seven years old, and he still needed them to show the way. She loved him so, if Mary was his choice, she would help him all she could. She felt in her heart, he had made a big mistake, but then Mary was young and perhaps she would improve with age.

Her quiet afternoon had come to an end, as she heard her other children come in the backdoor chattering at each other. Fred had taken them over to Wayne and Irene's to make plans for a Christmas Party. Dorothy had been in a good mood, until she heard the news of the elopement. "Why did he have to go and marry her of all people?" She shouted, and stamped around the room. "She acts so stupid most of the time, and she wears such hideous clothes."

Anna knew Dorothy loved Leonard, and didn't want a favorite brother married to anyone. He had always been a good brother and put up with her more so than Wayne had. She hadn't made a fuss when Wayne eloped with Irene. Anna started pulling pans from the cupboards, "let's get supper started, they're coming back here in awhile to eat with us and spend the night. What's done is done, so let's just make the best of it!"

Dorothy stayed out of Mary's way and ignored her as much as possible, trying to follow Mom's advice and make the best of it. She had a headache the night before, so she had over slept. When she came downstairs to the kitchen, she found that breakfast was over and the kitchen empty. Her place was still set however, and food had been left for her in the warming oven. She had just sat down to begin her meal, when Mary entered the kitchen, carrying the chamber pot from their room. She stopped at the big kitchen stove and took the lid from the pot and placed it on the top of the stove. Dorothy looked on, in disbelief, of anyone doing such a thing. Then Mary took a large ladle of hot water from the reservoir at the side of the range and poured it into the pot. Steam poured from the pot with the odor of urine enveloping the kitchen. Dorothy began to gag, and then she became enraged. She jumped up from the table, knocking over her chair, in her attempt to reach Mary. One hand grabbed a handful of bobbed hair, and with the other she gave Mary a hard slap to her face. She pulled Mary to the floor and continued to beat her in a rage.

Anna came running to the kitchen when she heard Mary's screams, and Dow hurried in right behind her. They pulled Dorothy to her feet and helped Mary from the floor. Dorothy was still shouting at her, "I'll teach you not to bring a piss pot into the kitchen when I'm eating breakfast!" Dorothy took note of her Mom then, "She put a pot lid on the stove Mom; she stunk up the whole kitchen. I'm going to beat the hell out of her everyday she's here!"

Anna took Dorothy into the parlor to calm her down, and Dow sent Mary upstairs to their room to fix herself up, then he went to the barn to find Leonard.

He explained to Leonard what had just occurred, "son, you must find a place of your own now. This is Dorothy's home until she marries, and now that you have married it's up to you to be on your own and take care of your wife." As it all worked out, Mrs. Kendrick gave them her house. She was tired of living alone, and moved in with her daughter and Ollie Tharp. Anna was relieved to see them go; Mary had been getting on her nerves. She had been trying her best to make the best of the situation, but she couldn't have held out much longer.

CHAPTER 23

THE GRANDCHILDREN

In March of 1928, everyone in the family gathered together for Anna's fifty-second birthday. She enjoyed her cake and opening her gifts, and then Mary announced her news, "You're going to be a Grandmother. I'm going to have a baby the first of October." Irene wasn't pleased at this, "well, of all things! I was planning to tell my news; I'm having a baby also in October." Anna laughed, both of her daughter-in-laws expecting at the same time. She was going to be busy sewing for both of them. First babies needed a lot of everything.

All through the summer, Anna made baby clothes, hemmed diapers, and made baby quilts, making sure each got the same amount. Irene was busy herself, getting prepared, but Mary was going about as usual, not doing much of anything. Her household was never neat and orderly. Food was served from whatever can was handy. Her dress was in disarray, with her slips hanging several inches below her dress. Anna was relieved to know that Mary's mother planned to move in and help, when the baby arrived.

The baby arrived on October first, a fine baby boy, they named Joseph. Anna and Dow made a visit to see their first grandchild. Leonard opened the front door that led directly into the small parlor. Anna couldn't see much, the room was so dark, with green blinds pulled down over the windows. She hated green blinds and dark rooms. Leonard rolled up the blinds and let the afternoon light in. Anna could now see that the room was the same as Mrs. Kendrick had left it. An old organ took up most of the space on the left side of the room, while the stove with a rack of drying diapers took up the right. Anna sat down gingerly on the old sofa hoping it would hold her weight.

Leonard brought out the baby to them, "By Jove! Don't he look just like me?" Anna reached out for the baby. "He is a fine boy; I know you're proud of him." She asked about Mary's health, being Mary was still in bed. A nine day period of bed rest being was the custom of the time, after giving birth. They made it a short visit, Anna was anxious to be out in the sunshine again.

Wayne and Irene's daughter arrived ten days later. They named her Violet. A visit was made again by Anna and Dow to see another grandchild. Margaret didn't have any children, and Anna didn't pry, into what she felt wasn't her business. Margaret was very social, she liked good times and parties. She traveled quite a bit with her prominent friends. One of these wealthy families owned a casket company, and the business seemed to require a lot of traveling. The wife wanted to go with her husband, so Margaret was asked to take care of the children for them.

Margaret could see right away, that the children did not have much of a home life. The first place she took them was to the family farm, to visit her parents. Anna was just putting dinner on the table when they arrived. She quickly added places for them to join their meal. Margaret filled their plates with meat, vegetables, mashed potatoes and gravy. Richard, the six year old, wrinkled his nose and asked, "What's this stuff?" As the dinner was being described to him, his sister Rosemary interrupted, "We can't eat this." Anna asked them, "What are you used to eating at your house?" "We have sandwiches, ice cream and cake," replied Richard. "We don't have any of that today, so it's eat what we have, or go hungry." said Anna. She didn't believe in catering to precocious children. Everyone went on with their dinner and ignored them. Richard picked up his fork and sampled the mashed potatoes and gravy. He took a larger bite the next time. Rosemary watched him, and she timidly began on hers also.

When Dow arose from the table he said, "I'm going to go out to the cornfield with the horses and wagon. Would you like to come with me Richard?" Richard said, "Yes," and followed him out to the pasture. There stood two of the biggest creatures Richard had ever seen. He watched Dow lead them to be harnessed and hitched to the wagon. Dow lifted him up to the wagon seat, and climbed up after him. Dow picked up the reins and slapped them against the horse's big rumps. Off they started for the fields beyond.

"What are their names?" asked Richard. Dow pointed to the big horse on the left, "That's Kate, and the other is Belle." Dow saw Kate start to lift her tail, and he knew what was going to occur. He thought he would have some fun with this youngster and initiate him to farm life. As Kate began to expel her load of horse droppings, Richard's eyes grew large at the sight. Dow shouted, "Get the plug," and Richard looked about him for something that might look like the item Dow was asking for. When the incident over, Dow laughed, and informed him that it was a natural occurrence for the horse. The children went home happy that evening, with the new experiences of the day, and asked if they could come again. This began a relationship that continued throughout their lives.

Times were changing, and not for the better. The country was in a depression, farm prices were down. Dow told Anna they would have to tighten the budget. Margaret and her husband were leaving their farm and moving to town. Joe wanted to manage a "filling station," as they called it, a place for gas, automobile parts, and the service the cars required. They bought a house on South Eighteenth-Street and Anna helped her to settle in. Anna knew they might be in for some rough times, but she knew they wouldn't be hungry. At least on the farm, they had a big garden of vegetables, and she always canned a lot for winter. There were always plenty of milk and eggs.

Margaret was also well provided, with Anna's fresh churned butter, milk and eggs from the farm. Margaret preferred the city life and her round of friends. She always brought her friends to visit Anna. Anna loved company, so this was enjoyable to her. Her world was expanded by the interesting people who entered her home. The parents of Richard and Rosemary had heard so much about Anna, from their children, which they met her and became close friends. Anna was a good listener; she enjoyed hearing of their travels and the business world in manufacturing caskets. They made her a blanket chest at the company. It was of oak, lined with cedar and decorated with brass and copper casket handles on each end, a very unusual piece. Anna was delighted with her gift and placed it at the foot of her bed, and into it, went her very best linens.

Margaret also introduced Anna to the Jones family of Whitewater. Doctor Jones and his wife had sons that had a funeral parlor in Richmond. This is what brought about Margaret's strange request. Margaret hurried into the kitchen, "Mama, I need a baby sitter." Anna gave her a strange look because Margaret didn't have any babies. "I'm going out with the Jones' this evening and they need someone to watch Gwen, their little girl. Their usual sitter is ill. Do you think Dorothy would do it?" She's in her room, go and ask her," replied Anna. When Dorothy had listened to Margaret's hasty explanation for needing a baby sitter, she asked, "are you bringing the little girl out here?" "No" Margaret hedged, "We will take you to their home and bring you back." "Isn't their home a funeral home?" asked Dorothy. "Well, yes it is," answered Margaret, "But there is no one there now, bodies I mean." "Do you think they would mind if I brought a friend to keep me company? I'm sure my friend Audrey would go," asked Dorothy. Margaret agreed to the plan hastily, she didn't want her evening spoiled. "Okay," said Dorothy. "It will probably be spooky there, but I'll do it."

Dorothy and Audrey found the home beautiful, and little Gwen was a darling. After a few stories, she was ready for bed. It had started to rain, and then the thunder and lightning began. "I hope the lights don't go out, it's kind of creepy as it is," Audrey commented. "Speaking of lights, reminds me, that I have to go put the outside lights on," said Dorothy. "Where do you have to go?" asked Audrey, not wanting to be left alone. "It's down at the end of a flight of steps at the back," answered Dorothy. "I'll be right back."

A dim bulb lighted the passageway and Dorothy made her way carefully. She had just started down the steps, when all of a sudden, a noise and something white, was coming fast up the steps towards her. It almost tripped her and she caught the handrail and sat down hard on the step. Her heart was pounding, and she felt as if it had skipped a beat. Then she saw what it was, and she laughed with relief. It was Gwen's big white Angora cat. She continued her way to the light switch, and said to herself, "what a night to spend in a funeral home, of course of all times, there would be thunder and lightning." On her way back to the front of the house, she saw a room full of caskets. This was the display room for people to pick from. She got an idea and went to get Audrey to see how she would react to it.

She brought Audrey back to the casket room and said to her, "I'm going to climb in a casket and you can tell me how I'm going to look when I'm dead." She stretched out in one, Audrey said, "you look fine, now get out, it's creepy." When Dorothy got out of the casket she said, "you know, they look like they would be nice and soft, but they're hard."

Margaret handed them each a dollar, from Gaylord Jones, on the way home in the car. "Look Audrey, we're rich and we had an experience we won't ever forget."

The school hack stopped at the end of the lane and Dorothy came running, banging the front door in her rush. "Mom, guess what happened today?" Anna met her in the front hall and led her into the parlor. "Well, come in and tell me what you're so excited about." Dorothy began, "A woman came to school to whip the teacher. We were sitting at our desks and the door suddenly opened and there she was, this woman in a black coat. She came in carrying one of those black snake whips, and started yelling at the teacher for stealing her husband. She chased her around the room trying to hit her. We tried to help the teacher by blocking the aisles, but that old crazy women lashed out with the whip and it caught Fanny Anderson across the shoulder. It cut through her dress, slashed open and she was bleeding. Fanny is a pretty good sized girl. She grabbed that whip and jerked it away from the woman, and she told her she was going to be in big trouble when she told her daddy about what happened. The old woman was scared then, but by that time, the Principal was there. I think one of the kids slipped out and got him. Our teacher left and someone else came in, but we were too excited to study. Somebody took Fanny home to get her cut taken care of. Everyone says she's a hero for what she done."

Anna nodded, "That was a brave thing to do, that's for sure. The woman must have been out of her mind to do such a thing, going to the school like that. What is this world coming to?" That was the topic at the dinner table that evening, with Dorothy happy to be the one with the news of the day. Dow shook his head, "You would think that school was the safest place for your child, I'll bet Jim Anderson is fuming over Fanny being hurt. I know I would, if it had been one of mine. He'll take action over this, you can be sure of that. We're just lucky that crazy woman didn't have a shotgun instead of that whip. "Oh, my Lord," gasped Anna, "I never thought of that."

Anna looked out at the frozen countryside. She turned to Dow seated at the table, in the warm, cozy, kitchen. "I hate January; it's the worst month to get through. It's always a let down after the Holiday season. I look forward to spring, to get outside and tend the garden."

"Well, I've got to go outside and get to the barn to see how Kate and Belle are doing this morning, Jack and Jenny too. I'm going to make them all some warm mash this morning." Dow got up from the table and began putting on his heavy coat, and pulling down the flaps on his hat to protect his ears from the biting cold. Anna called after him, "Tell Virling to come inside, he's shoveled enough snow."

Dow opened the kitchen door to find Wayne standing there. "We didn't hear you drive up." Anna called to him, "come in and warm up, you must be froze, out on a day like this. I'll get you some hot coffee." Wayne entered the warm kitchen, and started unbuttoning his coat. "I can't stay long. I came to get you Mom; Irene had the baby last night. We got a boy this time. Her sister Tootie is with her right now, but she would like for you to come and see the baby." "Have your coffee, and I'll be ready in a jiffy." Anna started to her room for her warm coat, scarf, hat and gloves. "My, how your days plan could change in a hurry." She was excited to go and see her new Grandson.

The roads were icy and lots of snow covered the countryside, but Wayne was a skilled and careful driver and Anna settled back to enjoy her ride. It was a beautiful morning. The snow sparkling with the sun shining on it and the pine trees glistening with the snow on their dark green branches. She had to admit that winter could be beautiful at times too.

Wayne's farm came in sight. Everything was neat and well kept. The house looked warm and inviting, smoke coming from a chimney on each end of the red brick house. Anna knew the inside would be neat as a pin also, for Irene, was a very good housekeeper and had a talent for decorating. She made her own draperies, slipcovers and bedspreads, taking pleasure in creating a lovely home for her family. Wayne had been very fortunate in his choice.

They entered the cozy kitchen, to find Tootie feeding, fifteen month old, Violet her breakfast. She was a pretty little girl, and she was getting excited at seeing her Grandma. "Eat your breakfast like a good girl. I'll be back in a while," Anna told her. Irene was resting after her ordeal. "You look well, and happy," Anna told her. "I am happy," Irene answered, "happy it's over with." She pulled back the covers, at her side. "Come see your new Grandson, isn't he cute?" She offered him up for Anna to hold.

Anna took him, in loving arms, and sat in the rocking chair

by the bed. "He is a darling, what are you going to name him?" "We have decided on Duane, Wayne didn't want a junior. What do you think of that?" Irene asked. "I think that's a fine name for him." Anna snuggled him close and rocked. The years passed, but she still hurt for her little boys that she lost. It was good to hold a baby in her arms again. They didn't stay infants long.

Irene seeming to know her thoughts of the past brought her back to the moment by asking, "Well, what's been going on lately? I've wanted to talk to you about Margaret. She's taking that teenage friend she met, into her home, to live with her and Joe. I don't think it's a good idea, I think she's making a big mistake." Anna nodded, agreeing with her, "I know, she told me the young girl has been pushed from pillar to post and hasn't had a home. You know Margaret, always wanting to take in every waif she meets, but I don't think it's a good idea either." "I tried to tell her, the last time she stopped by; I trust my husband too, but why put temptation in his path? She's just looking for trouble as I see it." Anna agreed with Irene's statement, and she knew Irene was watchful where her husband was concerned, and where she had been at one time herself.

The baby started to whimper and the little hands to push against her. "This little fellow is getting hungry, so I'm going to let you take care of that, and I'll be getting back to fix dinner for the family. I'll make extra today and send some over." "I'm so glad you came, come back soon," Irene said to her. Anna told her she would, and went to play with Violet before leaving. This was one household she didn't worry about.

CHAPTER 24

MARGARET'S MARRIAGES

Anna went outside to look over her garden. Spring was on its way at last. She was anxious to see what had survived the cold winter. She looked toward the lane as she heard a car drive up, and saw it was Margaret. The car door slammed and Margaret came marching across the lawn in a hurry. Anna could tell she was distraught over something. Before she reached her, Margaret called out to her, "Come inside Mama, I need to talk to you."

Anna settled herself in her favorite chair, in the parlor, and Margaret took a chair close by and began to cry. "I've lost him Mama, I've lost Joe! I'm so mad; I don't know what to do. I walked in on them unexpectedly yesterday, they were kissing!" Anna didn't need to ask who, she had misgivings about Margaret taking the young girl into her home, and now those fears had come to pass. She asked, "Who was kissing who? Maybe she was kissing him and he was innocent on his part." Margaret stormed, "I don't care who started it, and they both looked guilty when I walked in, I'm through, and I'm getting a divorce!"

Margaret was seldom at home, going off with the Jones family on trips, or with the Watt family to be a nanny for Rosemary and Richard. Anna remarked to Dow, "She seems to have recovered from her heartbreak mighty fast." Margaret started bringing a new fellow by and was introduced as her friend Bob Murphy. They spent evenings with the family, entertaining them with duets played on the new piano, which Margaret had brought out to them from her home in town. It was also a player piano, and played piano rolls operated by foot pedals.

Dorothy had been playing the piano rolls, when she got up from the bench and doubled over with pain. "What's the matter, something hurting you?" inquired Dow. "Yes, my side hurts," stated Dorothy, clutching her lower right side. "She probably ate too many pickles," said Joann. "Stretch out there on the sofa and rest, and see if the pain eases up," Anna told her. When the pain continued, and increased after an hour had gone by, Anna told Dow to go for the doctor.

Reid Memorial Hospital

It was the doctor's opinion that a surgeon be called in on the case, and for Dorothy to be taken to Reid Hospital. His diagnosis was Appendicitis! Margaret sat with a very worried Anna in the waiting room of the hospital. "She'll be alright Mama, I've heard this doctor is very good," encouraged Margaret. "I don't know, I've heard of cases where they've died of this," remarked Anna.

The doctor approached them, still in his surgical gown. "We were too late." Anna clutched her heart, and as the color left her face. The Doctor realized he must clear this up for her in a hurry. "I mean we were too late, the appendix had burst, but the operation went fine. She will have to have a drain tube in and her recovery a bit slower, but she will be fine." Anna then recovered herself. The color returned to her face, and she could speak, "When can we see her?" "In a little while, she's coming out of the ether we gave her now."

Dorothy was in a ward, with four beds to a room. The beds were white enamel, with a crank at the foot to adjust the position. Her bed was in a prone position, with her flat on her back. A glass tube from her side was draining into a glass jar under the bed. Anna thought she looked deathly pale. "This child has been through so much illness, Diphtheria, Typhoid Fever, and now a burst appendix. Lord, look after her, I trust her to you," she prayed. Dorothy recovered, and was able to celebrate her Eighteenth birthday in style. She also left the hospital with a nursing career in mind for herself.

Margaret decided to take Dorothy out for a special evening with her friends. They drove to Dayton, Ohio to a fancy Supper Club for dinner and dancing. Margaret requested a table along the dance floor, and it was also nearest to the orchestra. From here, they had a fine view of everything going on around them. The orchestra leader was dressed in a tuxedo with tails, and black patent leather shoes, with a very high gloss. The music was lovely, and the dinner delicious. The evening was going perfect, until the dessert came.

Dorothy had ordered Lemon Meringue Pie. It was a beautiful slice, the meringue stiff and piled high. She brought her fork down, and the crust was hard and unyielding, the pie flew from the plate and landed face up, almost under the feet of the orchestra leader. He was unaware of how close he came to stepping in the pie as he moved leading the music with his baton. Dorothy watched each and every step he took, waiting for that awful moment when those beautifully shined shoes would come in contact with that pie. It was a miracle, it never happened. Intermission came, the orchestra took their leave, and a janitor cleaned up the pie.

Margaret greeted the family with the news that she had married Bob Murphy and that they were going to California to live. She was only taking her clothes, so she asked to leave her belongings there with them. Anna said to Dow that evening, "She's just married him to get to California." "Well, times are changing and maybe she will be better off there." This gave Dow a good opportunity to speak to her about a change for them. "We need a place closer to town, I can't keep up the way I used to. Leonard told me of a nice big home next to him that's available. It has barns and plenty of garden space." "Let's go look at it Dow." Anna knew the time would come when Dow could not keep up the farm by himself. Fred had a job in town that he liked, but he helped work on the farm too, and that didn't give him much time for himself.

Anna thought the house was perfect for them. It had a large front porch and lovely yard. It had a front parlor, as well as a large living room. The Dining room had built-in china cupboards, and double windows that faced Leonard's home across a wide garden area. The stairway was closed; a door in the dining room led to the upper floor with three large bedrooms and a large floored attic room. "Let's take it Dow, you would have a nice barn for Kate and

Belle, and Jack and Jenny too." Anna added that feature, knowing that would close the deal. Anna settled happily into the house on North-West Fifth-Street. Leonard was happy to have Mom and Pop next door.

House on North-West 5th Street

Times were indeed changing; Wayne sold his farm and bought a lot just up the street from Anna and Dow. He built a new Cape Cod style home. He took a job with one of the new factories that had come to town. Cards and letters arrived each week from Margaret in California. One letter informed them of her divorce from Bob Murphy. "Didn't I tell you? I knew he was just her ticket to California," Anna told Dow after she had read him Margaret's letter.

Fred could devote all his time to the service station now. He was interested in cars and bought a nice one for himself. He had always taken Anna and Dow where they wanted to go, he knew Dow would never learn to drive or own one. Virling rode his bicycle around the neighborhood, never venturing too far from home. He did all the gardening, except for Anna's special roses. Dorothy began nurses training at Reid Hospital. She spent the week nights at the nurse's home, and came home on weekends. She entertained Anna with stories of what went on, in the busy hospital everyday. She worked very hard, but it was what she liked.

Dorothy talked Fred into teaching her how to drive the car. Her first attempt took out the garage doors, but she soon mastered it and became a good driver. It was a help to Fred because she took Anna to do her shopping on Saturdays.

Margaret continued to send cards and letters, sometimes enclosing a pretty handkerchief for Anna or a few dollars, which Anna just stashed away in her drawer. Another letter from Margaret, told the family that she had married again. "He was the love of her life." He was a Virginian that had come to California and he owned his own service station there in Wilmington. That's where she had met him; she was starting a hamburger stand across the street. His name is Earl Eaton, so address her mail to Margaret Eaton from now on. Joann standing by listening to the letter said, "Gosh, this makes her third one!"

Dorothy took Anna home after her shopping and drove to Shera's Service Station on South Fifth Street to pick up Fred from his work. She parked the car and went inside. The counter was lined with boxes that contained wall clocks in a variety of colors. Fred was looking one over, and another clock was being examined by a very handsome dark haired man. He was dressed in a gray suit, complete with matching vest. He looked up and nodded his head to her in a way of speaking. Fred said to him then, "Bob, this is my sister Dorothy," and to Dorothy, "This is Bob French, he comes around once or twice a week. We're looking at these clocks they sent, we're going to give them away as premiums with purchases. Dorothy picked up a yellow one, "I like this one." Bob smiled at her, "I buy a lot of gas here, I can get that one for you." Fred informed her, "Bob has two trucks, as well as that "35" Ford out there." He was trying to give her a good hint. Be on your best behavior, this guy is a good "catch." His good looks and clothes were enough to attract her, so she was glad to continue a conversation and get to know him.

Robert French

In the following weeks, she made it a point to be at Shera's at the right time, in hope of seeing him and she usually did. He asked her out on dates, and picked her up at the hospital or at her home. Anna liked him from the first time she met him. He was quiet, well mannered, a true southern gentleman, because he was from the South. He told her he came from Friendsville, Tennessee, a small settlement in the foothills of the Great Smoky Mountains.

Anna discovered more about this fine man as time went by. He told her he had been married before. His wife had passed away two years ago. He also had had a child, a baby girl; they had lost at two weeks after her birth. He owned a home not far from them and his sister-in-law and her family lived with him. Anna's heart went out to him even more; he had known the sorrows that she had.

Joann liked him and hoped Dorothy would marry him. She would like him for a brother-in-law, but to Dorothy, she would say, "Hurry up and get married so I can have our room all to myself!"

CHAPTER 25

DOROTHY ELOPES

Dorothy walked into the sunny kitchen and removed her hat, gloves, and winter coat and placed them on a chair. She had on her nurse's uniform; she had waited to change at home on Saturday morning as she usually did on weekends. It was early February, clear and cold.

"How did you get home?" asked Anna. Dorothy replied as she started for the stairway, "Bob picked me up at the hospital." Anna reminded her as usual, "I'll be wanting you to drive me to town today." Dorothy laughed, "Not today Mama, I'm getting married today!" Anna turned to go back to the kitchen, "Yes? Well, it takes two to make a bargain!" Awhile later she heard a car pull into the driveway and Dorothy came into the kitchen to get her coat. "See you later Mama," and she was out the door.

Anna asked Fred to take her to the A&P store, when he came home for lunch. She did her shopping in a hurry so she wouldn't keep him away from the station long. After putting her groceries in the pantry, she started preparations for their dinner. She set the table with her set of Blue Willow china. She set a place for Bob, thinking Dorothy might ask him to stay for dinner. They hadn't returned yet, and it was close to dinner time. They didn't arrive, so the family of five, as it was now, sat down to enjoys the food.

As the evening wore on, Anna began to be concerned that Dorothy wasn't home yet. Dow sat by the library table reading his newspaper, Joann was working a jig saw puzzle, and she was trying to darn some socks. She saw the lights of the car through the front room window as it turned into the drive and gave a sigh of relief.

Dorothy came in the front door with Bob behind her, hurrying to close the door to keep the cold air out. Dorothy went straight to her mother's chair and held out her hand. A gold wedding set shone on her finger. "I told you I was getting married today." Anna put her hands to cover her face and burst into tears, "First Margaret, and now you, Isn't there ever to be a proper wedding in this family?" Wiping her tears, she looked across the room and saw Bob looking very uncomfortable. Somehow she knew, he would never do anything to hurt her for the world. She went to him and took him by the arm and led him to a chair, "Come in and join us while I see what Dorothy's up to next."

Dorothy was going up the stairs to her room. Anna joined her there. "Now, how did this all come about so sudden?" asked Anna. "He said, let's get married, and I said yes. I couldn't wait, there's this other girl that's after him. She tries all kinds of little tricks to be with him. We had a date, and she begged him to drive her to New Castle to meet someone, so he agreed to take her. She thought he would break our date, but instead, he asked if I would like to take a drive up to New Castle, and minded if she rode along to keep her appointment. She was sure surprised, when she saw me in the car when we picked her up. Then she ran around to get in his door, so she could sit next to him, and put me by the window. Bob told her she was in my seat, but she just laughed and didn't move. I said, "That's alright there's more scenery to see by the window and let her sit there. She kept talking all the way there. We pulled up to the place where she was to meet someone, but nobody was there yet. Bob got her out of the car, and since it was a nice eating place, he told her he was sure they would be along soon and we must be going. Later that evening he said, let's get married." Anna thinking back to a red haired woman in a buggy said, "I see what you mean."

Dorothy started packing a suitcase, "We're going to Tennessee to see his folks for our honeymoon, and while we're gone, his sister-in-law and family will be moving out of the house, so we can settle in when we get back. Anna followed Dorothy and Bob to the front door and wished them a safe journey.

Later that night, as they talked about the new marriage, Anna explained things to Dow as Dorothy had explained them to her. "I like Bob, he's such a gentleman and very good looking, Dorothy's lucky to get him, after all, she's twenty-eight years old and about time she was getting married." Dow reminded her, "He's been married before, but I suppose enough time has gone by since she passed away." "Fred likes him, he told me he always pays cash at the station and seems to have plenty of money," Anna informed him. Dow patted her arm, "Well, let's get some sleep, we have a new son-in-law and we'll get to know more about him as time goes by."

Dorothy picked up Anna in Bob's Ford automobile and drove the few blocks around to her new home. "I want you to see the house Mama, and help me set up housekeeping in it." The house was located in a new section, as Benten Heights on the deed. The street was graveled and only three houses had been built so far on that street. The house was a bungalow painted cream trimmed in white, with a front porch across the entire front. Dorothy unlocked the, paneled glass, front door with a skeleton key and they entered directly into the small living room. "I'm getting new furniture, I picked out a maroon couch and matching chair." A wide cased opening, with a large drapery rod intended for portieres, led to the dining room, with a swinging paneled door to the kitchen. "These green cabinets are being taken out, I can't stand them, and Bob said he would put them in the basement for storage."

Dorothy led the way to the bedroom to show the new bedroom suite that had arrived. It was a new modern style with a low dresser with a huge round mirror. The bed had coil springs with mattress on top. Dorothy had a set of white sheets and pillowcases in preparation for making the bed, along with a chenille spread. "It's just these four rooms?" asked Anna. "Yes, for now," replied Dorothy. "Bob is going to add more later and put in a bathroom." Returning to the kitchen and looking out the back door, she saw a sidewalk leading to a garage painted cream to match the house, and the little "out house" also. "I wonder why they didn't add a bath when they built this house as new as it is?" said Anna. "Look how long they've had toilets, tubs, and sinks, well, as long as I can remember in the plumbing shop of my Papa's. Let's go along home now so I can get some supper started for all of us. You and Bob might just as well have dinner with us; your kitchen isn't ready to cook in yet. I remember how it was with my kitchen when I was a new bride. That big black iron range was quite a chore. Dow had to keep a pile of wood chopped to keep it going so we had hot water in the tank along one end of it, they called it a reservoir. You can just light your oil stove whenever you want a flame for a burner."

Dorothy locked the front door and they started off for her former home. "I'm glad we're close by, so we can still do things together, there's a household auction sale next week. I want to go and perhaps find a few things I can use. I know how you enjoy going to a sale Mama." "I do love to get a bargain." agreed Anna. They had the outing all planned by the time they reached home.

Dorothy's nursing career was cut short by pregnancy. Anna watched her carefully, making sure she rested and ate plenty of the fresh vegetables from her garden. They spent the summer afternoons making baby clothes and hemming yards and yards of material for diapers.

Fall came, with its beautiful colored leaves and crispness to the air. Crops were gathered in and the last of the garden produce brought in, to be stored in the cellar. It was Sunday and Dows birthday. Anna was putting the finishing touches to his birthday cake. "Wouldn't it be nice if Dorothy had that baby today on your birthday?" Anna asked. "Yes, it would, Joe and Violet came close," he answered. Anna had planned a special dinner with everyone in the family coming: Leonard, Mary and little Joe from next door, Wayne, Irene and their two, Violet and Duane from just up the road, and Dorothy and Bob just a few blocks away. She was so fortunate to have her family close. Fred had asked for the day off at the service station, and Virling and Joann were at home to help her with the dinner.

Virling had become a big help to her. He hung the wash on the line, did all the yard work and gardening with plowing and cultivating. He helped wash the dishes and clean the floors. "Had this been Gods plan?" She thought, "The others leave me, but I'll always have him by my side."

The dining table was set with Anna's blue willow china. She had roasted chickens, her own, large, fat, leghorns. Anna made her own stuffing, and placed bowl after bowl of delicious food upon the long table. She had decorated his birthday cake with candy pieces that spelled out "Happy Birthday" that she had found on a cardboard square for just that purpose at the A&P store. She added a few candles; there was no way for that cake to hold "Seventy Five." "We're getting old," she thought. "Where has the time gone? It's strange, I don't feel old, but let's face it, I'm Sixty Three now. Dow is really showing his age. His hair is snow white, but his dark eyes still have that sparkle. We've had a good life together in spite of our age difference. Mama and Papa had worried so about that."

Dorothy entering the kitchen broke Anna's thoughts. "I didn't hear you come in, have you been here long?" "Not long," Dorothy replied. "We were talking to Irene and Wayne in the living room. Irene wanted to know when I was going to have this baby." "Well, she should know that they come when they're ready." Anna laughed, "I don't think she's ready to have any more. Those two have been enough for her."

Everyone enjoyed the dinner, and then the lighted cake was brought to the table. Dow blew out the candles, and said to Anna, "You've outdone yourself Anna, the big meal and this fancy cake, but then, when haven't you been the one to go all out for us on every occasion." He opened his gifts and a special evening was enjoyed telling old stories over again. They all knew they were going to hear the mule story, and sure enough he bragged on Jack and Jenny coming back home again.

By ten o'clock, everyone had left and the kitchen had been put in order. Anna and Dow climbed the stairs to their room. It seemed to Anna, that she had just gone to sleep when she was awakened by a knocking at the door. Dow went downstairs to answer the door. He had an idea who it might be, and sure enough it was Bob. "Dorothy wants her Mom. She sent me to get her and go for the doctor." Anna quickly dressed and Bob put her in the car and drove the short distance to his home. As soon as he got Anna into the house, he took off to get the doctor. Dorothy was propped up on the sofa, in the living room, covered with a blanket. "You're not having the baby there are you?" inquired Anna. "No Mama, I've got the bed ready and everything laid out for the baby, all sterile," Dorothy answered. "Why didn't you go to the hospital?" Anna wanted to know. "I know those girls, they would play some trick on me, and Bob would be so uncomfortable at the hospital."

Anna settled herself in the matching chair to the sofa, and asked, "Which doctor is Bob going after?" "Doctor Busche, I told him how to get there." They heard steps on the porch, the front door opened, and in stepped Doctor Huffnagel. "Well," he said brusly, "Are you going to have the baby there." "No!" she said, getting up from the sofa and going to the bedroom. Anna could see that Bob was upset. "Sit down Bob, she's going to be alright." "I got the wrong doctor, I got on the wrong street and couldn't find the address, so I got this one," Bob confessed. "That's alright, she knows this one too from the hospital," Anna consoled him. Anna knew he was nervous; he had lost a child, so that made this one very precious. The hours passed slowly.

The doctor opened the bedroom door and motioned for them. "It's a girl, and I would say she's an eight pounder!" "You can get her dressed Grandma." He handed the baby to Anna. Anna took the baby loosely wrapped in a receiving blanket. She opened the bundle of sterile wrapped clothes. Bob hovered at her side looking on at his new daughter. First Anna put on the gauze belly band to protect where the cord had been severed. Next came the flannel diaper carefully pinned, then a shirt and a soft flannel gown. She was placed in a pink blanket, to swaddle her in, and she was put in her Daddy's arms for the first time.

He held her very carefully and handed her back to Anna. He went to see Dorothy and pay the doctor. The baby girl was named Elisabeth Ann. Elisabeth for a little girl Dorothy had taken care of in the hospital and grew very fond of, and Ann after her Grandmother Anna.

Bob took Anna home. Dawn was breaking on a new day as he pulled in the driveway. "Thanks for being there," Bob told her. "I'm glad I was there to pin on her first diaper," Anna said. "Little Ann," as the family began to refer to the new baby, was welcomed by everyone in the family. Gifts were brought or sent, especially by "aunt" Margaret almost every week.

A letter came from Bob's sister in Tennessee announcing that her baby girl had been born on the same day, and hoped they would be bringing the baby for them to see. Anna and Dow began to take more of an interest in this baby. Everything was more fun, all of her "firsts," her first Christmas, Easter and everything else that came along. Dow would babysit when Anna and Dorothy went shopping.

CHAPTER 26

ANN

A telegram was delivered to Bob on a summer evening as he sat on the porch swing with his little Ann. Dorothy came out on the porch, "What's wrong?" A telegram was always bad news. Bob handed her the yellow sheet of paper. "Lizzie's baby is dead. She died with Spinal Meningitis. We have to go to Tennessee tomorrow for the funeral." "I'll run over and let the folks know we'll be gone for a few days." Dorothy got the keys to the car and set off.

Anna felt sorry for the family; she knew what Lizzie was going through. She couldn't settle herself down to sleep. A sudden thought came to her, "What if their baby should catch the dreaded disease, and they were taking her right to the place where the sick baby had been. Why didn't I tell them to leave her here with me? I must go and get her first thing in the morning before they leave."

It was just past dawn, when Anna started across the field she used as a short cut to Dorothy's house. When she saw the house closed up, she knew she was too late, and she sat down on the porch steps and cried. She worried everyday until the day when Dorothy came driving up and brought the baby to her. "We got back late last night; it's a long day's drive."

Anna hugged the baby close, "I was so worried, I went to your house early to get her and found you had left. You took her into a bad sickness. What did Bob's folks think of her? Anna asked." "Well, she was passed around from one person to the next, and all I heard was, "So this is Bob's daughter," Dorothy said with a sneer. "You would think I didn't have anything to do with her at all!"

They said little Ann was the "spittin" image of her daddy. He carried her everywhere with him, and except for the times she was with Anna and Dow, she was never far from him. He was teaching her to spell and learn at an early age, and Anna saw he was also teaching her right from wrong and to share.

Little Ann also loved her Grandpa Dow, and he adored her. As soon as she was big enough, he put her behind Kate and Belle with the reins in her hand, and she drove the team, with him behind, holding her.

Dow went to town one day, which he didn't do often. He came home with a pair of little black boots with red tassels. He showed them proudly to Anna, "Won't she be something in these? I'm going to take them over to her right now." A short time later, Anna heard Dow slam the door behind him and stomp into the kitchen. "Dorothy won't let her have the boots; she took them away from her with me standing right there. The little thing was happy with them, I could tell, she was trying to get them on her feet and laughing."

Anna shook her head; "I don't know what gets into her sometimes." Anna never missed much that went on around her. She saw the way Dorothy treated her child sometimes, and she noticed it was always Bob, that Ann ran to. Anna had also seen

Dorothy slap Ann when she was just a baby in her buggy and the people around them had frowned at it, she had told Dorothy what she thought, but when had that ever made a difference with her. "I'm going to get her something else, and I just dare her, to take it back!" as Dow stomped out to the barn.

The next day, Dow went to Rohe's Jewelry Store on Main Street and purchased a tiny gold locket on a thin gold chain. He took it home to show Anna, and then took the path across the field to Dorothy's. Without any preliminary conversation he simply stated, "I went back to town and got her this necklace, and you had better not be taking it back!" Dorothy could tell he was still mad, so she smoothed it over, "Well, this is more what a little girl should have, I won't take it back." Dow gave her a glaring look, "I know you won't, because you don't have the receipt!" He turned his back and started home.

Ann climbed up on Grandma Anna's lap, "Tell me a story Grandma." Anna cuddled her close, how she loved this child! She began a favorite story for her.... "Come in little stranger, I said, as she tapped on my half open door. While the blanket pinned over her head, just reached to the basket she bore. I asked, what's your name little girl? Tis Mary, she said, Mary Doll, as she carelessly tossed off a curl that hung on her delicate brow. A look full of innocence fell from her pretty blue eyes as she said, I have matches to sell and hope you are willing to buy, a penny a bunch is the price, I think not too much. They are tied up, so even and nice and ready to light with a touch. My father was lost on the deep, the ship never got to the shore. Mother is sad and will weep to hear the wind blow and so roar. She sits there at home without food beside poor sick Willie's bed. She spent all her money for wood, so I sell matches for bread. I go to the yard and pick up chips, but it would make me so sad, to see the men building ships and think they had made one so bad. But God, I am sure that takes fatherly care of a bird, will never forsake a child who trusts in his word. Fly home little bird then, I thought. Fly home full of joy to your nest, for I bought all the matches she brought and Mary may tell you the rest."

Anna had always loved that story; she looked down and found that Ann was sound asleep. Dorothy stayed close to her folks, and many evenings after supper they would go there for a short visit. They spoke of what was going on in town, or what was in the newspaper. Bob mentioned that the property directly behind them was in line with the gravel pit that he hauled from, it was for sale, and he was going to buy it. "I think it's a good investment," he stated.

As Anna was preparing for bed, Dow suddenly said, "I think it's a good investment too. I think I'll buy it myself." "What," asked Anna? Dow repeated his words, "I'm going to buy that gravel pit." Anna was stunned, "You have never bought a piece of property in all your life, why now?" "Because," Dow said, "Bob said it was a good investment." Anna looked at him, "He also said he was going to buy it." "Not if I buy it first!" Dow stated. Anna put her hands on her hips and looked him in the eye. "That would not be fair! You will turn him against this family, and I like him. He trusted you with his plans. He could take our granddaughter away. She is exactly like him in every way. She is her Father's Daughter; if you wrong him you wrong her too!"

Her plea fell on deaf ears, because the next day Dow and Fred went to buy the property. Anna worried and wondered what was going to happen when Bob found out. Bob never showed any indication to them that the incident ever happened. What he truly felt they never saw a sign. When Dorothy had told him what they had done, he said, "It's my own fault, I should never have told them my plans, and you can be sure it won't happen again." He told Ann about it when she was a grown woman and would understand, and perhaps learn from it, and be wise enough to keep things to yourself.

CHAPTER 27

THE LAST DAYS

The Japanese attacked Pearl Harbor and the U.S. was at war! I went through other wars, but this one has hit me personally. I'm Sixty Seven years old today and I don't have enough sugar to bake a cake, that is, if I was inclined to bake one. There is no butter, this white stuff they call Oleo is a poor substitute. Joann has no nylon stockings and gas is rationed for the car. What next? Next was the white envelope that came in the mail with Selective Service on it addressed to Fred. Anna cried, "Surely they won't take him, he has a crippled hand, he's too old, he's Thirty Seven. He's our only support, what can we do?" Dorothy tried to console her, "He has to go for his Physical is all, they may not take him. Bob had to go for his and he was turned down because of his rupture. I'll drive him over to Cambridge City to catch the bus and you can go along. Your worry may not happen." But it did, Fred was accepted and sent to Fort Lewis, Washington.

He was made an M. P. Anna worried about him, and she also had Dow to worry about. Dow was failing everyday. Her friends and neighbors decided to take matters into their own hands and they contacted the Red Cross. This was a case where the man was needed at home. Red tape takes awhile to straighten out; Fred was onboard, ready to ship out, when the orders came for him to go home. Anna was so thankful to have him home safe, and to all those who helped bring him home.

The doctor sent Dow to the hospital, but Dow wouldn't stay. He ranted and raved, dressed himself and insisted on going home. The doctor made calls to the house, left medicine that Dow wouldn't take, and day by day he got weaker and could not leave his bed. The family watched over him night and day.

Anna looked out at the lovely April day. "Spring is here at last, I want to open those windows by the bed so Dow can feel the fresh air." They had put his bed in the dining room, in front of the double windows so Dow could have a good view of the garden. "I also want Kate and Belle brought to the window so Dow can see them. That would brighten his day." Fred nodded, "I'll do that right away."

Dorothy and Ann were coming in the door, they went to Dow's bedside, and Anna joined them there. She thought Dow looked bad today. His face was almost as white as his snow white hair. She went to open the windows and Kate and Belle came up to the windows at that moment. "Look Dow, here's two old friends to see you this morning." Dow turned his head to face the windows, and a warm smile lit up his face. He reached a feeble hand out as if he could touch them. "My best friends look after them." His lips moved but his voice was so low that they leaned down to hear what he was saying. "Little Ann?" "She's right here Papa," Dorothy told him. "Take care of Ann," he said. He was talking but they couldn't understand him, "I'm walking on the water, I'm going to be all right," he whispered. Anna asked them, "What does he want? Some water?" "No Mama, he's gone from us, and I think he was telling us he was crossing over. He's with Jesus now." "I knew the time was near but I wasn't ready to let him go." She looked down at the still form of her beloved. A flash of memories came flooding back to her. His dark eyes looking up at her as he adjusted her skate, and smiling down at her as he put her wedding ring on her finger. She looked up at the windows, to see Kate and Belle still standing there, quietly looking on, as if they too, were in mourning.

Relatives and friends came to give their sympathy and support through her time of sorrow. The funeral was overseen by the Jones family; again Margaret did not come home. The hearse proceeded to Lutherania Cemetery on the Liberty Pike, through the gates and around the circular chapel, passing the many gravestones, tall granite shafts and quaint tablets from a century before. The trees were beginning to bud, and a cold, April, wind whistled through the tall, dark, green, pines.

Anna and her children gathered at the graveside. Ann was holding tight to her Daddy's hand. Dorothy was helping Aunt Myrtle and Uncle Matt to a nearby chair, and keeping an eye on Joann for fear she might faint again. Joann was taking her Papa's death very hard. Anna's mind had a hard time taking all this in, she was thinking, "This can't be happening, what will I do without him?" Then a restful thought, "The boys will have their Papa again." Before she was ready to leave, the service was over and she was led away from the graveside. She tried to look back to tell him, "I don't want to leave you Dow, but it seems I must."

Her life had changed, once she had taken care of them, they now took care of her. Fred was the head of the house now. He worked and supported her, as well as Virling and Joann. Virling was a very good housekeeper. He reminded her of an "old maid" with his fussy ways. He was plumping up the pillows before people were hardly off them. He had learned to cook from watching her all those years, and that was a good thing because Joann was going to marry a nice young man from Ohio.

They were going to live at the old place until Fred had the new house finished. It was to be a modern house with all the rooms on one floor, no steps for Anna to climb. Anna sat on the front porch, writing her letters of thanks, for the flowers that were sent, and all the other tokens sent in sympathy to her of Dow's passing. She received a lot of mail each day, and she answered her mail promptly. Telephones had become very popular, but she couldn't have the expense of one. Margaret still wrote every week, still giving excuses of why she couldn't come home to the funeral. She still sent a few dollars each time, and Anna still just put it in her drawer.

She began to be excited about moving into a new house. She had moved so many times in her lifetime, but never into a brand new house. Anna, Fred and Virling moved to their new home. The modern bathroom next to her bedroom was so convenient for her. The new electric stove and refrigerator in the cheerful kitchen, with rows of windows making it light and airy was a delight. She also had a telephone in the house, and wonders of all wonders, a television set. She could now see the actors of her soap opera's instead of just listening on the radio. She even enjoyed the commercials.

Ann had her own television set at her house, but she still came to visit often, bringing news of school and neighborhood happenings. Best of all, Dorothy was allowing her to have a dog finally. It was a black cocker spaniel and she loved it. Anna was happy for her, to have this companion, an only child is often a lonely child, and she knew Dorothy wasn't always pleasant to deal with.

Summer of 1955, Anna became confined to her bed. Ann spent afternoons reading, talking, and listening to her Grandma's stories. She arranged the roses in a vase on the bedside table, but without Anna's care, they were not as abundant as they had always been. Anna noticed the lavender cotton full skirt Ann wore, with the bouffant crinolines under it, that was the style of the time. "I like that color of your skirt," she said to her. "When I die, I'd like a scarf of that color for my neck." "Oh Grandma, don't talk about dying, but you shall have the scarf."

In September, Ann had to return to the High School for the fall semester. One afternoon Dorothy rushed to school to get her, Anna was dying. As the family gathered by her bedside, Anna spoke to them, "My sister Caroline was here today." Ann looked at her mother with a questioning look, "How can that be? Caroline had been dead for years. Anna was the last of her line." Anna looked at the open window, a warm breeze stirred the lace curtains, and she asked, "Who are all those people out there?" Ann looked to see, and she saw no one there. When she looked back to her Grandmother, she saw that Anna had died.

Fred reached over and closed her eyes for her eternal sleep. He removed the gold ring from her finger and put it in Ann's hand. "She wanted you to have this." Ann clenched her fist around the ring in her hand, and her tears blurred her sight. She would treasure this ring just as Anna had all these years and pass it on to her Granddaughter someday.

The visitation and funeral was at the Jones Funeral Home. When Ann entered the room, banked with flowers, and approached the casket, she saw the lavender scarf was in place. Anna didn't need it to hide the lumps on her throat from the goiters, they were gone. Her throat was smooth, and her face was the way Dorothy remembered her looking when Dorothy was a little girl. Ann was amazed at the throngs of people that came to pay their respects and sign the quest book. In attendance, were the lives that Anna had touched over the years, the rich and elite of Richmond, to the very poorest.

As Ann was introduced, and heard the stories of how they knew Anna, she came to realize that even though she had never left Richmond, she was a very great lady. The organ was playing softly; it was Anna's favorite Hymn. Ann closed her tear filled eyes and listened, she remembered Anna singing softly to her, "I Come to the Garden Alone, While the Dew Is Still on the Roses."